Once in Old Frisco

Once in Old Frisco

by Elaine Egbert

♥

AUTUMN HOUSE® PUBLISHING COMPANY
P.O. Box 1139, Hagerstown, Maryland 21741-1139

Copyright © 1991
Autumn House Publishing Company

The author assumes full responsibility for the accuracy of all facts and
quotations as cited in this book.

This book was
Edited by Penny Estes Wheeler
Designed by Bill Kirstein
Cover illustration by Joe Van Severan
Type set: 11/13 Times Roman

PRINTED IN U.S.A.

94 93 92 91   10 9 8 7 6 5 4 3 2 1

AH Cataloging Service
Egbert, Elaine.
    Once in old Frisco.

    I. Title.
        818.54

ISBN 1-878951-09-2

Dedication

I dedicate this book to
my husband, Bob,
who knows just the right thing to say when I get writer's block,
who did first-hand research for me
while he was in San Francisco during the 1989 earthquake,
and who has gone out of his way to create time
for me to pursue my hobby of writing.
His willingness to let the characters ''live with us''
while they are being put on paper is deeply appreciated.

Acknowledgements

Thanks to my uncle Carl who kept me spellbound as a child when telling about his experiences during the 1906 San Francisco earthquake; to Joyce Van Scheik and Keith Clouten of Canadian Union College library for their help in confirming details; and to Dr. Terry Graham for sharing his historical wisdom with me.

"Faster!" yelled Karl as he dashed ahead of Enoch down Modesto's board sidewalk and tore around the corner of Mason's Mercantile. The two boys' feet drummed a hollow tattoo against the weathered boards in their frantic attempt to avoid the hateful Thornton brothers. "C'mon!" Karl urged, hoping Enoch's short legs could keep up with his longer stride.

Across the alley they darted, past Miss Minnie's with her outlandish display of ladies' hats. Now only Ralleigh's Fine Meats lay between them and the country road—the beginning of their own territory.

But it was no use, for suddenly the dreaded brothers jumped from Ralleigh's doorway and blocked the walk. Unable to dodge the older boys, Karl skidded to a stop so fast that Enoch plowed right into him.

"Well, lookie there, Ez," Sid sneered, exposing his square yellow teeth. "If it ain't them smelly farm boys hurryin' home to milk their precious cows!"

Enoch grabbed Karl's arms from behind. "It don't m-matter what they say, K-Karl," he panted. "Jist don't f-fight again."

As though controlled by one mind, the Thornton brothers stepped forward in their store-bought shirts and britches and peered over Karl's shoulder at Enoch. "Wanta see yer fancy boots, runt," Ez sneered. He swiped Karl aside like he was no bigger than a suckling pig, then pointed at Enoch's feet. "Funny yer Pa couldn't make better boots 'n' that, seein's he useta work in a cobbler shop!"

Sid, the larger of the two, shook his head in mock sympathy, his eyes dancing in delight. "Look at them clumpy heels—and them uneven lace holes. I'd be 'shamed to have them on my feet."

Anger, bitter as overgrown dandelion greens, filled Karl's mouth. He'd had enough of the Thornton brothers taunting his friend! How dare they make Enoch's life so miserable?

Karl's heart pounded a warning as he stretched to his full height and glared up at Sid. "Must make you feel real brave, picking on fourth-graders," he chided.

Ez spun around, the well-known warning look in his eyes. "Watch it, kid. Sid wasn't talkin' to you. Sides, he ain't doin' no harm. Just wants to see them fancy boots E-e-enoch wears—that's all."

Runty in his worn overalls, Enoch slouched before the Thorntons' mocking stares. Then Ez jabbed Enoch's middle. "S'pose you 'splain how yer Pa made them fancy boots."

Karl glanced at Enoch's feet—feet much too large for his puny body. The over-sized boots with their thick soles and square leather lacings were well-worn and stained.

"Speak up, boy," growled Ez. "Don't 'cha know it's rude not to answer when spoken to?"

Enoch drew a shuddery breath. "H-he t-t-took—"

Karl could bear it no longer. Everyone in town knew how shy Enoch was—how hard it was for him to talk to folks. They knew how his tongue jumped around, making him stutter when he got nervous. From the beginning Karl had been Enoch's spokesman. Lately he'd been his protector, too.

With a roar, Karl leapt onto Ez, knocking him against the meat market wall and then onto the board walk. Cursing, Ez shook Karl off and picked himself up.

"Yer gonna be sorry you did that, dwarf!" His spidery fingers bit into Karl's shoulder, clinging—twisting. "Say yer sorry!"

Karl held his breath against the searing pain and refused to cry out! Instead he doubled up his fist and let Ez have it right in the gut!

Just then an arm wrapped around him from behind. He twisted and as the sharp sound of ripping cloth filled the air he caught a glimpse of Enoch's pale face and gaping mouth. Then he landed on the splintery boards with Sid's foot right in his middle.

"Guess you ain't learned yer lesson yet," spat Sid, glaring down at him.

Blind fury erased Karl's fear as he struggled to free himself. He was tired of the Thorntons picking on younger kids every night after school! Tired of them saying farm boys were no good. Why, he wouldn't be a town boy for anything in the world! Milky-faced fellows with nothing better to do than make life tough for hard-working lads who wore hand-me-downs and sometimes stuttered! He didn't care what happened. Didn't care if he went home with a black eye again! He was going to put a stop to Thorntons' pestering, once and for all, or die trying.

"You leave Enoch alone!" he bellowed, glancing a blow off Sid's chin.

On the sidelines Enoch called out, his thin voice piercing the scuffle. "Fer'git it, K-Karl. 'Taint w-worth it!"

A heavy wallop floored Karl, and for a moment he lay in a heap, gasping for breath. Then, eyes glued to Sid's sardonic grin, he struggled to his feet again.

At that moment a new hand grabbed him. "Hold it!" ordered Mr. Ralleigh who still wore his butchering apron. He plunked his other meaty hand in the middle of Sid's chest and clamped on. "What's the trouble?"

A few minutes later Karl limped down the county road

toward home, Enoch at his side.

"It don't m-matter what they say 'bout my boots—I know they's good 'uns," Enoch declared. "I 'preciate yer standin' up fer me, but it ain't worth the p-poundin' you always git. Jist lookit' yer n-nose! An' yer shirt is tore."

Karl's whole face throbbed, and each thud of his heels on the dusty road vibrated through his swollen lips. He pressed his hand over them to give them more support, but even that hurt. Finally he stopped and faced Enoch. "How can you let those guys push you around like that?"

Enoch shrugged. "Fightin' back ain't gonna stop 'em from p-pickin' on me. Sides, I know my boots look funny. Even Pa says so. But they feel right fine 'n' that's all what counts." He scuffed at a stone. Karl watched it kick up little puffs of dirt as it skidded along.

"But—"

"Pa says gettin' mad is lettin' other fellers take control of you. They eggs you on 'til they g-git you in their power." Enoch shook his head. "I sure don't want them guys controllin' me!"

It was a disturbing thought. Karl had accomplished nothing but a bloody nose, a pair of banana lips, and a ripped shirt. And anger still seethed through him. The Thornton brothers had cooked up some fancy story for Mr. Ralleigh, then went off laughing up their sleeves. They'd probably be waiting to torment him and Enoch again tomorrow night.

"Maybe if we both jumped them ahead of time—made a good plan, or something," Karl suggested.

"Fightin's wrong," declared Enoch, his blue eyes peeking from beneath his scruff of stiff yellow hair. "Good Book sez so."

Karl heaved a sigh. What was the use? Enoch always talked about the Good Book, like it was something more than a fancy set of fairy stories. Himself, he leaned more to the way Pa felt—that religion was only for old ladies and weaklings. That people who cottoned to religion always stood back and let other folks fight their battles. Yep, Pa was right. But he liked Enoch and his family anyway. There was something special about them that he couldn't quite name.

"Well, if we're not gonna fight 'em, we've gotta find a way to outsmart 'em," Karl mumbled, gingerly touching his nose. "Question is how."

That evening, after Ma had worked on his face, Karl joined his family at the supper table. No sooner had the spuds, beans, and the platter of hogback made its way around all eight places than everyone dug in.

"What's this Ma was telling me about the Thornton boys?" Pa asked after the younger children had stopped chattering.

Karl chewed carefully, moving his lips as little as possible. "They were poking fun at Enoch's boots again."

"Look at Karl's face," Ma cut in, her voice filled with concern. "This is the worst they've done him yet. And his shirt is ripped beyond repair!" She turned to Karl. "Can't you avoid those boys?"

Karl wedged another spud into his mouth. How could he explain to her?

"Comes a time when a man's gotta stand up for his rights," Pa declared.

A warm feeling spread through Karl as he met Pa's gaze. Pa didn't cotton to fighting either, but he understood how it was to survive in a world of bigger boys—that you couldn't always run. That was one thing about Pa. He always knew how things stood. He was strong, but careful at the same time, and Karl vowed to be exactly like him when he grew up.

He glanced around the table. Concern filled Ma's eyes —concern for his puffy face, not his torn shirt. Ma—always willing to do for her family without even a "thanks" in return.

He eyed the others too—his three younger brothers who

looked to him for an example, and two little sisters who hung onto him whenever they were close enough. This was his family. They all had each other—he didn't have to go out on the street like the Thornton brothers and torment others to make himself important. It was evident by the faces that surrounded him that he really did belong. Not for all the money in the world would he ever leave the farm—or his family. He'd stay here where he was wanted, tending the farm and living with the people he loved until he dropped dead as an old man.

Karl watched Ma go to the pantry and retrieve two fat apple pies. It would be hard, but he'd eat every bite of his share. He looked up at Ma and pulled his lips into a wobbly smile.

Two summers later Karl leaned on his hoe and wiped his shirtsleeve across his forehead. The blue sky, brilliant and without a smudge of cloud, promised a scorcher of a day, even though it was still early June. From where he stood the long rows of beans Pa had set him to weeding stretched toward the barbed-wire fence. If he didn't get moving, he'd still be in the bean patch come noontime.

At last sixth grade lay behind him. He smiled at the thought of the long summer ahead. No more books. No more trying to outsmart the Thornton brothers, and no more being cooped up in a desk he'd outgrown—not until autumn came and the harvests were finished. He sniffed the warm, clear air, glad just to be alive. In spite of dawn to dusk work he loved the farm, the dewey mornings, the heavy sweetness of the pasture grass on a hot evening, and the cozy feeling that he got when the whole family worked together to make their place the best one in the valley.

Bending to his task once more, he listened to the hoe's metallic chuff as it nipped off the weeds. High above, a crow screeched as it circled in an effort to escape a pestersome flock of black birds intent on protecting their territory.

Hoeing faster, Karl grinned to himself. Pa had promised that he could go to Enoch's after supper if he finished his chores early enough. Out of school for two weeks, he'd missed the easygoing relationship he and Enoch shared. Besides, Karl wanted to see how Schneider's orange orchard was doing. Seemed like growing an orchard might be less work and much more profitable than growing corn like everyone else did.

He tried to imagine how the field would look with rows of orange trees and their clouds of sweet-smelling blossoms in the springtime. Later the deep green foliage would be dotted with yellow balls that gradually turned setting-sun gold.

A warm glow washed over him. He'd never forget the time a couple months before when he'd been standing in this very spot trying to figure a quicker way to do their spring planting. Pa had even stopped his work to listen to his ideas.

When Karl had finished, Pa draped his arm across his shoulders. "Boy, you're a natural-born farmer. Since you're the oldest, this farm will be yours someday. Come that time you'll have to make many decisions—decisions that will affect the whole family." He went on to tell Karl many things he thought he should know. Then he gazed out over the sleeping land and sighed.

"Guess the time has come for you and me to work on a man-to-man basis. Then when you take over you'll already know what you need to know."

"But I'll do things the same way you do, Pa," Karl insisted.

Pa squeezed Karl's shoulder. "I know, boy."

It felt good to have Pa's trust, and the realization the land would someday be his own made Karl work harder than most 12-year-olds he knew. He didn't want the place to himself, or for Pa to get too old to work, or anything. But it would feel good to carry on the family tradition of crop farming, just like Pa now did.

After Karl finished hoeing and had mended the Eastside fence he cut across the fields to Enoch's place. Mrs. Schneider, short and plump, met him at the door.

16

"Lookin' fer Enoch?" she asked, waving him inside with her wooden spoon.

"Yes'm. Want to see the oranges."

"Ach!" she grinned, her cherry cheeks squeezing her eyes into merry slits. "And it's all the time he's out there, too. You want a cookie?"

Karl's mouth watered as Mrs. Schneider took a cookie sheet from the woodstove oven. "New preacher's comin' to town Sunday," she continued as she slipped them onto a plate. Then she poured a cup of milk and put it on the table. "Havin' a basket dinner right after the service—fried chicken 'n everything." She touched his arm. "Why'nt you come along? Hear tell Reverend Flemming's a right good talker."

Karl eyed the cookie plate. It was really something how Mrs. Schneider always invited him to church no matter how often he declined. Matter of fact, the whole Schneider family seemed determined to get Karl inside those four walls and, according to Enoch, "into the fold of God."

He reached for a cookie and took a swig of milk. Once when he was littler he'd asked Pa if they couldn't start going to church, but Pa just laughed.

"God does nothing for people, my boy. People have to do for themselves. Man wastes lots of time in those clapboard churches, singing and praying, when he should be out using his hands to feed the hungry." He tousled Karl's hair. "Long as you're good to your neighbors and honest in your dealings, that's all that's required of man."

Karl smiled at the gentle woman who waited hopefully for his answer. "Thanks, Mrs. Schneider, but we're pulling stumps on Sunday. Nice of you to ask, though." He gave her a quick hug and then trotted off to find Enoch.

When he spotted Enoch at the orchard's edge he gave a whistle. Enoch whirled and dropped his shovel. "Tarnation!" he yelped. "I didn't 'spect to see you 'fore Independence Day!"

Karl closed the space between them, then cuffed Enoch's shoulder. "Come to see your trees before they're full grown!"

He scanned the slope which dropped away toward the creek. The trees spread like an emerald carpet right down to the water's edge. Here and there amid the leaves hung green walnut-sized oranges.

Enoch grinned. "Give this here orchard a year or two. We'll get a zillion oranges offen them trees, mark my word!"

Karl sighed. "Wish Pa and me would plant a starter crop in the bean patch."

The boys discussed Karl's idea as they wandered through the grove, inspecting the trees. Later, when the shadows lengthened, they turned toward Enoch's house, falling silent in their warm comradeship.

Enoch 'n' me, we'll always be neighbors, Karl mused, remembering how they'd been best friends since first grade. It didn't matter to Karl that Enoch was a head shorter and scrawny compared to his own robust size. It didn't matter that Enoch looked 10 while Karl looked 15. They'd lived next door to each other forever. They were buddies. He just wished they had more time to spend together when school was out, but it couldn't be helped. That was the way life was for farmers.

The summer passed quickly, filled from sunup to sundown with mending fence, hoeing corn, baling alfalfa and milking tail-swishing cows. There was scarcely time to think about Enoch, let alone going for visits. And then it was September again, and once more the friends met each morning for the long walk to the schoolhouse.

Now a new schoolmaster reigned in the three-room school, a man straight from San Francisco. With his snappy city clothes and worldly knowledge, he not only took his students into his heart, but he took them on mind travels as well. Right there in their desks, surrounded by chalk dust and the fragrance of newly-sharpened pencils, he escorted them from their rough-heeled farm community into the midst of the glamor and culture of big-city living.

As he described the blue bay waters, the salty early morning tang punctuated by sea gull cries, and the busy streets filled with snappy rigs, Karl's desire to see the city on the hill was born. "Might be fun to live in a city for a while," he suggested on his homeward trek with Enoch one late afternoon. "We could work for merchants—drive a nice rig."

Enoch shook his head. "I reckon Frisco'd be interestin' all right, but a feller'd never be happy there. Too many people—'n no quiet to think. No place to stretch out. And where'd a man plant his crops?"

Karl laughed. "City folks don't plant! They get their provisions in shops—go to work in an office or a store." He sighed. "And when the day's done they don't have to face a barn full of stubborn cows."

Just voicing his thoughts set Karl's imagination awhirl. "Just once I'd like to see that ocean. Imagine so much water you can't see across." He poked Enoch. "Did you hear Mr. Felder say that you can actually see the curve of the earth on the horizon? And the ships—"

"Sounds like you've caught a whoppin' case of itchy feet, always hankerin' to see what lies beyond the next rise in the road," Enoch interrupted. "Reckon if you keep talkin' like that you'll be packin' yerself off and turnin' into a citified dandy some day."

Karl toyed with the idea, then discarded it. Everyone knew it was the oldest son's place to help carry the burdens of the family. Knowing what he would be doing with his life had always been comforting. Yet suddenly he felt strangely annoyed.

"Reckon I'll never see anything but the farmland between here and the hills," he muttered.

But in school the studies of distant places, new inventions, and brand new ways to do things did not end just because Karl would always be a farm boy. One Friday Mr. Felder faced his students.

"Next week we will pair off to give oral reports on United States cities. Karl and Enoch will study how New York City is important to our nation. The reports will be next Friday."

Using materials Mr. Felder had supplied, Karl and Enoch studied together for the allowed hour each school day.

After listing everything that should be included in their report, Karl tipped back in his chair and ran his fingers though his curly hair. "Which section do you want to report on?"

Enoch licked his lips. "N-None. You know I can't talk up front."

Karl remembered the times Enoch had become tongue-tied while making a report. He thumped his pal on the back. "Don't worry. You're older now."

The following Friday as Karl and Enoch trudged through the misty morning Karl jabbered away just to keep Enoch's mind off the coming report. White-faced, Enoch hardly spoke a word, but plodded beside Karl, his eyes glued to the dusty road.

After lunch, Mr. Felder stood beside his desk and smiled. "Now Karl and Enoch will report on New York City. Perhaps some of you will be fortunate enough to visit there someday," he added wistfully, the way he always did when speaking of far off places. "Gentlemen, are you ready to recite?"

As he headed to the front, Karl visualized Enoch picking at his fingers like he always did when nervous. But Karl could hardly wait to tell the interesting things he'd learned. Time flew as he described the different nationalities who flooded to the city in hopes of finding a better way to live.

When he had finished, Mr. Felder nodded happily, making Karl's spirits soar!

It was a long moment before Enoch pried himself from his seat. His heavy boots clomped halfway up the aisle, then stopped. Without a word he retraced his steps, picked up his papers, and stumbled back toward the front. Finally he hunched behind the podium, his eyes never lifting. An uneasy silence settled over the room as the students waited for him to begin.

Enoch shuffled the papers on Mr. Felder's podium. He stood on one foot, then the other. He licked his lips, gasped for a breath, then licked his lips again. "Uh, I'm s'posta t-talk about—about—" His eyes sought Karl.

Enoch's nervousness reached out and grabbed Karl, like a fist clenching his middle. Karl nodded quick encouragement.

"—about w-work in N-new York."

A bead of sweat dribbled down Enoch's flaming cheek. He swiped at it, as though it were a pestersome fly. His eyes darted toward the door. Again he licked his lips.

"P-people hafta work."

Someone in the back of the room tittered. Karl stiffened as Mr. Felder glared at the offender, then took an encouraging step toward Enoch.

"And what kind of work did the New Yorker's find to do?" Mr. Felder prompted.

"Uh—there was bots of lilding."

The class exploded into laughter. Enoch's bloodless fingers clenched the podium. "I m-mean, there was l-lots of building. People coming. They had'ta have p-places to l-live."

Enoch heaved a shuddery sigh. Sweat glistened on his brow. He licked his lips. Again he tried, only to become more tongue-tied.

"Hey Schneider," hooted Sid Thornton who was still the biggest boy in the room. "Cat got'cher tongue or somethin'?"

The hair on Karl's neck stood up. How dare Sid poke fun at Enoch!

Enoch froze as his eyes fastened on Karl in a silent plea for help.

"Look!" hooted Sid. "It's the S-statue of L-liberty, standing in our own c-classroom. We don't need'ta go to New York!''

Again the classroom erupted with laughter. But Karl was not amused! Before he could think twice he shot from his seat, vaulted Enoch's desk and hurled himself at Sid. "You clam up!'' he shrieked.

His attack caught everyone off guard, and the two surprised boys tumbled to the floor amid a background of scuffling feet and screaming girls. A fist thudded against Karl's cheek as he scrambled to right himself and pin down the heckler. All the hate which had built over the years flamed through him now. At last he'd teach Sid not to mock Enoch!

Strong hands tried to pry Karl away, but he wouldn't let go. Sid writhed below, and finally managed to grab Karl's arm. He twisted. Pain, hot as a branding iron, shot through Karl's shoulder, but he wouldn't give up.

Then, amid the shuffle, a quiet voice pierced Karl's anger. "Let him b-be. He didn't mean n-no harm.''

Enoch had wedged himself between the desks, down beside the two struggling boys. "Come offen him, Karl. It don't m-matter none.''

Then Mr. Felder was there, pulling them apart. Karl's thoughts whirled angrily! Why couldn't they just let him finish his job once and for all? Frustrated, he shook the others off and bolted for the door.

The cool November breeze felt good on Karl's scalding cheeks as he flopped onto the schoolhouse steps. His insides shook like Ma's new jelly as he clenched his fists. It wasn't fair how that big bully picked on Enoch! Everyone knew how Enoch got, and most of the students tried to encourage him. Yet when Sid and Ez made fun of Enoch, sometimes the others laughed too.

"I'll get that Sid after school!'' Karl vowed. "That big bully's picked on Enoch for the last time!

Just then the school door creaked open and Enoch squatted beside him. "Thanks fer t-tryin' to shut Sid up," he began. "That feller' always d-did have it in fer me."

Karl stared at Enoch's boots, tracing the path of leather laces as they reached between the lopsided lace holes. Mr. Schneider never could seem to get them just right, and it made Enoch's feet awkwardly duck-like.

"I wisht I wouldn't c-clam up like that," Enoch ventured.

"Someday I'm gonna kill that Sid," Karl vowed.

Enoch picked at a loose thread on his knee. "Ain't worth th' bother. Can'cha see he's t-trying to get control of me—by pokin' fun? An' I'm not gonna let him. Pa says an angry man can't think straight—that the one he's f-fired up at is the one in control of things. Anger makes a man a p-puppet, he says. Guess Sid's gettin' control of you, too."

"He is not!" Karl yelped, leaping up.

Enoch didn't budge. "Is t-too. Makes you so's you can't stop yer'self from f-flyin' off. Then you get hurt or in t-trouble."

The air went out of Karl. Enoch was right. Sid was probably back in the room right now, gloating over what had happened. It wasn't the first time. It probably wouldn't be the last.

Karl grinned in spite of himself. "And you always come around and calm me down. Make me see straight again. Even if it's you he's picking on."

The color had begun to creep back into Enoch's face. "So? Lotsa t-times when I clam up like that you t-talk for me. Guess it's an even swap."

They laughed then, the anger and tension dropping away like fat green peas being stripped from their pod. Karl grinned over at his friend. It had always been that way. It always would. They would always stick together—watch out for each other, smooth each other's way. That's what friends were for.

Karl sloshed water from the enamel bowl onto his face, slicked a bit through his tangled hair, then pulled the rough hop-sacking towel from it's hook and dried. Late afternoon light slanted through the kitchen window as he replaced the towel, unmercifully exposing the face in the mirror.

He leaned forward and eyed the large red welt on the side of his nose. Beside it the smaller blotches across his face looked insignificant. Lately he'd been breaking out with such fiery spots. Nothing helped. It was just like the rest of his life—uncomfortable things popping up everywhere.

He leaned closer to pinch a spot on his cheek. The one on his nose hurt too much to touch.

"Don't pick at those," Ma warned as she hurried to the pantry. "You'll leave scars."

"It's my face," Karl mumbled beneath his breath as he moved to a spot on his chin. Beneath his fingertips stiff hairs bristled, making the job more difficult. He stopped his picking and ran his hand over his chin. Yes, there were more whiskers than there had been yesterday, a definite sign he was growing up. Already he took the razor to his face once a week, which was oftener than most 14-year-olds did. Try as he might, he couldn't hide his pride over the precious growth, even though Enoch sometimes called him "cactus face." Enoch had not managed to produce even one whisker yet and still looked like a kid.

"Let's eat!" called his oldest sister, Tildy, as she carried a bowl of hot vegetables across the kitchen.

Karl's stomach growled as he headed for the table amidst the scramble of brothers and sisters. Tildy elbowed her way through the swarm and set a bowl of cottage cheese on the table while Ma lifted little Bethene, the newest sister, into the same high chair that Karl and the other six had used.

When everyone was seated Pa looked around the table, acknowledging Ma and each child with a warm smile. "My, this supper smells good," he said, starting the meat platter. Then, as usual, Pa asked each of the children about their day, giving them time to be heard. Afterward, the banter flew back and forth as the children joked and teased together.

Ma and Pa joined in, and laughter filled the room, just as it always had as the family got down to the business emptying the steaming bowls of good food. But the peaceful feeling their togetherness had given Karl in times past now seemed strangely absent.

Karl glanced around the table. Everyone looked so happy— fitted in so well. Everyone except him, he thought, feeling the cold, hard spot deep inside himself that was so new to him. Puzzled, he drew into himself. How had things changed so much? When he was a kid he'd been so satisfied with his family's country ways. Nor had it bothered him that his parents lacked polish—even though Ma had once been a school marm and continually corrected their grammar and insisted that they keep up with their studies. Until recently it hadn't even riled Karl that Pa was reluctant to try new methods around the farm.

His thoughts returned to the past Sunday when he and his brothers had been walking the fence line with Pa and Stewie, discussing spring repairs. As usual, 8-year-old Hank behind tagged Pa, hanging onto every word, trying to copy Pa's long stride and manner of speaking. Karl glared at the pesky kid, uncomfortably annoyed that he'd been the same way about Pa—trying to be just like him, and all.

A tinge of something unpleasant had settled over him as he turned his back on the two and scrutinized the largest of their cornfields. At the time of earth's resting, it held nothing but leftover stubble from the winter. But soon another summer— blazing under the hot sun—would be upon them. He would again devote hours of his time to hoeing weeds that tried to choke out tender plants. Each year Pa planted corn and beans. Each year they grew—sometimes good, sometimes better. But at the end of summer, the crop was finished. The field sat doing nothing. Barren. Dry. And come spring they had to start all over again.

Karl remembered how he had faced Pa. "I think we should plant us a grove of oranges," he said, finally blurting out the idea he'd been toying with for a year.

Pa's face closed.

"It would cost a fair penny to get the trees set," Karl hurried to explain, willing Pa to listen. "But that would be it. Wouldn't have to keep putting in seed. Could get between them with the plow. Think of the spring work it'd save! Besides, everybody's growing corn."

Pa scratched his chin and gazed across the fence. His stiff whiskers sounded like dry cornstalks on a windy October day as he continued to fiddle with them. Karl knew he was thinking, and a tiny thread of hope began building deep inside him.

"Corn's always paid our bills," Pa finally said, turning back to the fence.

Karl faced him squarely. "But oranges are a better cash crop. Look how well Schneider's orchard is doing!"

Pa straightened up and faced Karl. "Son, I don't favor oranges. I like the turnover crops—ones that will give us cash every year. Cash we need. It would be several years before oranges paid their way, and what would we live on 'til then?''

Karl stiffened, and the words he'd held back for so long came gushing right out of his mouth! "But Pa, you're old-fashioned! How do you expect to get ahead, just doing the same old thing every year? Oranges will bring much more money in the long run. Anyway, what about what *I* think? You've always said this'll be my place. Don't I have any say in what its future should be?''

An expression Karl had never seen before slid across Pa's usually placid face, then disappeared. Suddenly Karl was aware of his brothers standing there, open-mouthed because of how he'd dared speak to Pa.

Pa took the pliers from his hip pocket and began fiddling with a loose piece of fencing. Silence, thick as a sod wall slipped between them as Karl waited for Pa's answer.

In school he had learned that one of the problems of older farmers was their reluctance to adopt better methods or try new crops. When Mr. Felder had said that it annoyed Karl, because he was sure Pa was the best farmer in the world. But now, watching Pa's reaction to a new idea, he wasn't so sure.

Finally Pa shoved the pliers into his pocket and faced Karl. "The matter's settled," he said flatly. "I've cared for this family so far, and I think I have a few good years left in me yet.''

Karl didn't know what it was—why those few moments out of all their years together seemed to get in the way of everything after that. Pa had never mentioned the incident again—had never spoken of Karl's hasty words—yet it hung between them. Karl's push for a say in things, and Pa's insistence that he was still in charge. Karl's growing annoyance at Pa's stubbornness was all mixed up with a sense of shame that he couldn't quite understand. It took over from the moment he opened his eyes in the morning, and haunted each waking hour, like a dismal mist sifting over everything he saw. It tinged every second of the day as Karl noticed other backward things Pa insisted on doing. Dismayed, Karl realized Pa could no longer be his model, and that things would never be the same again.

"Karl?"

Ma's voice jerked him back to the present, and again he became aware of the others as they downed their evening meal.

"Karl, eat your dinner."

Ma's gaze lingered on him, and it held a tinge of worry. Karl didn't return her smile but instead looked away. He still loved her a lot, but—. He sneaked another look at her. It was as though he saw her for the first time. Never before had he stopped to think if she was beautiful or not, for she was Ma, and had always been there. But what he now saw came as a shock!

Had she ever been a young woman? Had her hands always been rough and red? Had she ever had pretty clothes? Somehow, he couldn't picture her as a teenage beauty, with a slim waist and fair cheeks like the girls he saw in town each time he went on an errand. Her companionable softness had always been a comfort to him. Now he realized she was merely lumpy, though she kept her girth covered with a clean apron. Karl shot a disgusted glance Pa's way. Ma shouldn't have to work so hard. Why hadn't Pa seen to that?

Fully shaken at this new insight, Karl slipped away from the table, plate untouched, leaving the younger boys to squabble over his piece of pie.

"Karl?" Ma's worried call followed him as he headed for the room he shared with his brothers. His straw tick rustled beneath him as he lay back and stared at the ceiling, savoring the few minutes of silence left to him. Life sure was confusing. You couldn't count on anything anymore—nothing stayed the same.

The weeks and months passed slowly after that. As always, Karl busied himself with the farm work. Sometimes he and Pa almost recaptured the comraderie of the past, but more often his frustration over Pa got between them.

As often as possible Karl headed for Enoch's. There was something different there, though he couldn't really put his finger on it. Sometimes he stayed for supper, which he enjoyed execpt for the strange custom the family had of pausing before they began eating. Once Mrs. Schneider and Hope and Grace had put the bowls onto the white-clothed table, each person would find his place. Karl's was always beside Enoch. Then Mr. Schneider would say, "We will return thanks to our Provider," and everyone held hands all around the table—even Karl.

There was a ring to Mr. Schneider's voice as he thanked "the God Who so mercifully blesses us" for the food he and Enoch had raised with their own hands. He thanked God for the bread that Mrs. Schneider had kneaded and baked and sliced herself. It seemed a silly custom, but at least no one got a head start on the food like Stewie usually did at home.

Funny thing was, there was a difference in the Schneider home—a purpose everyone seemed to revolve around. Sometimes Karl wished his family had the same thing, but if it meant going to that stuffy little church in town—

One afternoon, shortly after school resumed, Karl labored over an arithmetic test. Only the scratching of pencils on paper disturbed the silence.

Then someone knocked on the door. Karl craned his neck to see who had come, but it was useless. Mr. Felder quickly answered, motioned for the students to continue their work, then stepped outside. A moment later Mr. Felder hurried to Enoch's side.

"You're needed at home," Karl heard him whisper.

Enoch shot a bewildered glance at Karl, then bolted for the door.

Karl touched Mr. Felder's arm. "What's wrong?"

Mr. Felder shook his head slightly, then turned to the class. "Please finish your work."

Puzzled, Karl stared out the window. A moment later he saw Dr. Graff's black buggy pull around the building. That glance was long enough. Inside the buggy, beside the gray-haired doctor, sat Enoch. From the back seat two white ovals peered out—the frightened faces of Hope and Grace, Enoch's little sisters.

Karl's heart lurched. If something wasn't terribly wrong Dr. Graff wouldn't have taken them out of school! Without a word Karl got up and headed for the door. He half expected Mr. Felder to stop him, but when he glanced toward his teacher, the man nodded silently, further clarifying Karl's feeling that something dreadful had happened.

Half an hour later he raced up Schneider's back steps. In answer to his knock the door opened a crack and exposed 9-year-old Grace's tear-stained face. Without a word she let him in. Stillness smothered the room as he waited for Enoch. A few moments later he heard his friend's shuffle on the stairs.

"I thought you might need me," Karl explained as Enoch hurried into the kitchen.

Enoch swiped a hand across his blotchy, swollen cheeks. "It's P-pa," he choked. "Somethin' weighing on his chest— can't breathe right. Dr. Graff says it don't l-look too good."

Something inside Karl jumped. "You mean—"

Enoch nodded. "But Ma 'n' me 'n' the girls have been p-prayin'." Hope flitted across Enoch's face. "God sez He answers prayers of them f-folks who love Him, and we're workin' mighty hard at believin'."

"But the doctor—"

Enoch shook his head as he turned to rejoin his family. "There ain't n-nothin' more he kin do."

Karl went outside and stood on the porch for a few minutes. How suddenly things changed! If Mr. Schneider died now, how would his family manage? Sure, Enoch was 14, but he wasn't ready to take over the farm! Of course, Enoch said they were praying for Mr. Schneider, and he knew they expected God to work some fancy miracle.

Karl shook his head. Strange how some people thought God would change things for them just because they asked. He shoved the thought away. Standing here on the back stoop wasn't going to change things, either. The least he could do was get a start on the chores so Enoch wouldn't have to shoulder everything alone.

With a sigh Karl headed for the barn, his mind full of ponderings that hadn't one single answer.

The next few weeks moved along with a steady rhythm. School without Enoch, homework, chores. When possible Karl slipped over to Schneider's to give Enoch a hand with his work. True to Enoch's declaration, Mr. Schneider started getting better, but his recovery was slow. Dr. Graff had said he shouldn't work as hard as before, so Schneiders decided to sell their orange grove. Not only would that lessen the work around the place, but it would provide some hard cash to help pay the mortgage on the rest of the land and keep the family going until Mr. Schneider could work again.

To Karl's surprise Pa decided to mortgage some of their land to buy Schneider's orange grove. Karl knew he should feel happy that they finally owned some of the emerald-leaved trees he'd longed to own, but it left a heaviness in his chest. As Karl worked in the grove with Pa, he couldn't forget the times he'd slipped over to Enoch's after his chores were finished and heard Mr. Schneider's strong voice singing praises to his God while pruning branches or loosening the earth around the trees.

But the loss of the orchard didn't seem to bother Enoch. "The Bible sez that ever'thing works together fer good for folks that love God," he said as he accepted his lot as farm chore hand while his pa recovered. Leave it to Enoch to bring God into everything that happened! Karl wouldn't be surprised if Enoch told him that the Lord actually came down and tied his boots each morning!

One afternoon Enoch faced Karl with a special request. "The church is holdin' a p-prayer service askin' God fer Pa's speedy recovery." His pale eyebrows climbed hopefully. "Sure would be swell if you'd c-come along."

Karl shook his head. "You know I don't believe, and I wouldn't want to ruin it for you. Only thing's gonna make your Pa better is rest and good food."

Disappointment flitted across Enoch's face. "God's promised," he said softly as he forced a smile. "You'll see."

Six weeks later they put Mr. Schneider into the ground. The ones he left behind stood in a tearful huddle, watching as the dirt sifted onto the wooden casket. For the next few evenings after school, Karl went to Enoch's place to help with chores. He expected Enoch to be long faced—to pull into himself as he faced the truth about the God who wasn't really there.

True, Enoch was sad, but Karl could see no sign of discouragement. "God had other plans fer Pa, that's all," he insisted. "He's not gonna f-fersake us jist 'cuz Pa ain't here no more. I got two strong arms, 'n' Hope 'n' Grace are big enough to help. We'll be OK, long as we k-keep our faith in God."

Karl wanted to shake Enoch! "But can't you see that God didn't do *anything* for you in spite of all your praying?"

Enoch hung his head and kicked at a dandelion. "Y'see, things ain't always c-clear to mortal man. But all's clear to God, 'n' we've put our lives in His hands. He ain't gonna let us down. You'll see."

Karl couldn't believe his friend. How foolish for people to think that there was Someone who helped you through life's problems! What wasted energy! It angered him to watch his friend fruitlessly wait for God to come in and fix everything. How could anyone be so dumb? Religion wasn't for families who were in real trouble—or for a young fellow who had suddenly become head of the household!

It was hard, but Karl swallowed his words and dug in to help Enoch with the milking that evening. As the steady white streams frothed into the pail between his knees, he knew that Enoch would be coming up against hard times. And when Enoch did, he'd be there to help—not God.

As winter drew on and the last of the crops were taken in, Karl made it over to Enoch's place less often. When he did he couldn't help but be amazed at the cheerful outlook of the entire family. Little Mrs. Schneider, always one for a cheerful word, beamed at him each time he came, giving him words of encouragement and stuffing him with cookies.

Karl had expected the uneasiness between him and Pa to vanish now that they had the oranges. But it didn't. Now Pa found fault with each thing Karl wanted to do in the orchard. It seemed as though he felt Karl was getting younger and less knowledgeable rather than older and more proficient with the many chores around a farm—and tree ranch.

"You've got to move slow in making changes, boy," Pa often said.

That slowness annoyed Karl. Didn't Pa realize that time waited for nothing? There were ways to increase land production, and it wasn't by standing back and letting the years pass. But Karl had been taught to swallow sharp words and to respect his parents. Acceptable youth simply didn't pop off and tell the older generation what they thought, like Karl had done once before. They must think of creative methods to show cautious oldsters a better way. So Karl swallowed his words and concentrated on doing things Pa's way, though impatience ate at him at every turn.

New Year's Day in 1906 would have been as ordinary as any other central California day, except that special festivities had been planned to dedicate the two rooms recently added to the schoolhouse. It had been bursting at its seams with children from new families who had moved into the community. Now there would be enough space to breathe during classes.

As one of the oldest boys in school, and no longer subject to whippings by the Thornton brothers, Karl stepped up to the flagpole with Mr. Felder, and to the background of two trumpets and a wheezy accordion, hoisted the flag that the schoolgirls and their mothers had created. It waved there, in the thin afternoon sunshine, showing off the carefully appliqued white letters on a green background—"Modesto District School, 1906."

The littlest children sang a song, and then there was a short explanation by Hope, Enoch's sister, about the colors of the flag. "Green stands for growing—which our school is doing. The white letters and numbers—they stand for purity of heart." She glanced at her ma who nodded her encouragement. "We dedicate our school—and ourselves, to the good of our community, and our land."

After hot chocolate in the schoolhouse, Karl and Enoch slipped away to talk. For a change Enoch seemed troubled.

"What's wrong?" Karl probed, never one to fiddle with small talk.

Enoch shrugged. "Gotta go into the bank tomorrow."

"The bank?"

Enoch chewed his lower lip. "M-mortgage payment's due and we don't got the money." His face twisted. "Y'know how I am, talkin' to folks. I get so flustered I can't line up two words b-back to back, let alone talk smooth enough to persuade the banker not to t-take our land!"

It bothered Karl to see Enoch so worried. Now that God was giving out on Schneider's, he must handle things. "Maybe I'll come along," he offered.

"You'd miss school," reminded Enoch.

"So what? I'll help you work something out with the banker. You'll see."

Never had Karl been so silver-tongued. To his delight,

Schneiders were allowed a three-month extension on their mortgage. To pay it off, Enoch decided to sell a few more acres. Then the place would be theirs—lock, stock, and barrel—and they wouldn't have to worry about losing everything.

That evening as Karl began milking, Jezebel was unusually ornery. First she refused to go into the barn. Then she wouldn't put her head into the stanchion until Karl coaxed her with an extra portion of meal. As he washed her udder she switched her tail and stomped. Finally Karl clenched the pail between his knees and settled down to business. Bell-like, the first streams of milk zinged against the naked metal, announcing "time to beg" to the barn cats.

As Karl got into the rhythm of milking his thoughts slipped to occupations Mr. Felder had been talking about in class—carpentry, engineering great bridges, medicine. What would it be like to do something other than farm all one's life? Pa was a farmer. Just like Grandpap had been. And Great Grandpap, for that matter. Karl was expected to be the same. He frowned. How did people ever get into different occupations if they had to follow what their fathers had done?

Jezebel stomped and slapped her tail across Karl's face. "Settle down, Jez," he grumbled, swiping at the sting.

If he could choose anything he wanted to do, he'd be an engineer and design skyscrapers for places like San Francisco! And with the money he earned he'd travel all over the world and see how other people lived.

The bucket was nearly full when the white streams became thinner. Karl wondered how long it would take to learn engineering. One had to learn a lot of arithmetic—that he knew. He had just begun stripping Jezebel out when the ornery old cow lashed out at him with her filthy back foot. With a clang she knocked the pail from between Karl's knees and sent him tumbling onto the messy floor. Stunned, Karl lay there like a sponge soaking up the warm milk, while the muck seeped into his clothes and hair.

An instant later he shot up and sprang at her, bringing his fist down hard between her shoulders. "That's the last time you'll kick me, you filthy bovine!" he yelled as he swiped the clotted straw from the back of his head. "You're no good for anything but meat on some beggar's plate!"

Alarmed, Jezebel thrashed in the stanchion, lashing out with her back leg again. Her amber eyes rolled wildly as she tried to free herself, but it was useless.

Karl glared at the hateful beast. Let her struggle until she slipped in her own muck and fell down! She could break her stupid neck for all he cared! The meat man would be glad to have her!

Karl fumed as Jezebel gradually quieted. And it was then that he knew for sure that he didn't want to be a farmer, now—or ever. In the past he'd been interested in what Pa called sowing, growing, and hoeing. But that was when he was too little to know there were other things a man could do. He'd been able to think only until harvest time when Pa came into the house with a mile-wide grin and his pocket full of dollars from the fall crops he'd just sold. Gratefully Karl would accept the silver dollar Pa pressed into his hand—not pay, but a reward for a year's good work.

Karl opened the stanchion. "I'm not going to finish strip-ping you!" he growled, kicking at her. "Get out of here!"

Karl picked up the bucket and milked the others, anger still chewing at him. Then he stomped into the house, sloshed water over his face, and stormed to the table.

"Whooee!" needled Stewie in his singsong way. "A storm cloud just blew in here." His eyes widened in pretended horror. "Pee-yew! What'd you get into?"

The other children joined in poking fun at their oldest brother. Karl endured it, tight lipped. Cows! Mouthy little children! He'd had enough of them all!

As Pa came in and dinner began Karl closed himself off from all of them. Finally they quit badgering him and the conversation turned to school and other less explosive things.

Then Amanda, who sat beside Karl, grabbed the bowl of greens and held it out to him. "Take this," she insisted, repeatedly bumping it against his arm.

He tried to ignore her, but finally his anger took over again. "I ain't hungry for no more!" he growled, savoring the poor English that poured from his lips.

"I'm not hungry for any more," Ma corrected gently. "Please speak carefully, Karl. Remember your influence," she added, with a meaningful glance at the younger children.

It seemed as though everyone and everything in the world was against him! No one cared how he felt! He wasn't even allowed to speak as he chose! Enraged, he exploded from his seat, sending his chair clattering across the floor just like Jezebel had done with the pail. He glared at Ma. "I ain't hungry no more for nothing, and I'll talk like I want!" he shouted.

Nine shocked pairs of eyes stared at him. Nine mouths dropped open, but no one was more surprised at his outburst than Karl himself. Before anyone could speak he stormed out of the kitchen. His feet thudded hard against the stairs as he fled to the bedroom he shared with his three disgusting little brothers. As he flung himself onto his cot he noticed that Ma had filled the tick with new straw that day. Somehow that made him even angrier. He took a deep breath and clamped down on the hard thing in his throat. Then he replayed the kitchen scene in his mind. It served them right! After all, who ever thought about his needs—his rights?

The following days became more and more difficult for Karl to bear. Amanda, now 6, tagged him incessantly, her nasal voice pelting him with question after question. Ralph ignored him. Stewie teased. Tildy scolded. Ma wore a puzzled, hurt look in her eyes, though she was gentle and never mentioned his outburst. Pa was the only one that acted like nothing had happened, and somehow that made Karl even angrier. Instead, in his quiet way, Pa continually reminded Karl that an eldest son's responsibility was to help take care of the family and to mind his example before them. The only place Karl found any peace was at school, where he literally buried himself in his books.

Evenings, as he milked, he let his mind wander. *Someday I'll get out of here—somehow. I'll go to Sacramento or better yet, San Francisco, and make something out of myself.* He thought about the long rows of corn that would need to be hoed come springtime. He thought of the endless fences separating their fields—fences that would need the usual mending. He thought of the prickly hay, and working long hours to bale it in the scorching summer sun.

"Whatever made me want to be a farmer?" he growled to Bertha, their stupidest cow, as he stripped her last drops of milk. Dread, heavy as an old wagon wheel, weighed him down. He'd never get away from the farm—not if he held up his end of the bargain with Pa.

As he thought of the long years ahead, his restlessness grew. He saw himself—an old man, still working their place, his brothers and sisters sapping off him, expecting him to provide for their every need. It was inevitable. He was stuck, and he might as well get used to the idea.

Later, while walking among the orange trees, he puzzled over the changes in his thinking. He had wanted this grove so badly! Now that they had it he wouldn't care if every tree died!

The clod he kicked exploded into a thousand pieces in the late afternoon sunlight. It was time to go home to supper. Home to be confronted by a circle of faces that would look at him in wonder, disgust and pain.

If only he could talk to Enoch! Enoch had a way of making

things seem better. But lately there hadn't been time to walk over after chores, not with darkness falling so early. Reluctantly, Karl turned homeward, feeling torn up inside. He longed for the unity he used to feel with his family. Yet at the same time he didn't care if he ever saw any of them again.

On Saturday while Karl cleaned the barn Enoch suddenly appeared. His obvious misery wrenched Karl's thoughts from himself, for silhouetted in the doorway, shoulders hunched and head bowed, Enoch looked forlorn and more vulnerable than ever.

Karl's heart lurched! Had someone else died? He dropped the manure shovel and hurried to Enoch's side.

"What's wrong?"

Enoch's lips had paled, and his troubled eyes fastened on Karl's.

"I got a f-fearsome decision to make," he stuttered, sagging against the barn door. "Y'see, I sold them three fields alright— Clancy O'Hare bought 'em. But I didn't get much fer 'em." He swiped the back of his hand across his eyes, and for a minute Karl was afraid Enoch was going to cry.

Then he straightened. "Trouble is, we had'ta add the rest'a our cash to the field money, 'n now there ain't enough left to see us through winter."

Shame crowded Karl. He'd stewed over lack of privacy and not being allowed to make his own choices while Enoch struggled for life itself.

"Ma's been real b-brave about it," Enoch continued. "She says the garden stuff'll be enough if we're right careful. But I know better. Pa—" his voice broke, "—told me once how much hard c-cash it takes to get through the winter, even if there ain't no extra expenses like repairs 'n stuff."

Karl touched Enoch's shoulder. "What'll you do?"

The thin afternoon sunshine filtered down, adding little warmth to the day. It glanced off Enoch's strawy hair and made a light spot against the weathered doorpost.

"Well, I gotta find day work somewheres," he said. "Ma 'n the girls'll hafta manage more of the farm work. Course there ain't much left to see to 'cept the milkin'. Hope says she k-kin do that if Grace'll help."

Karl thought for a moment. "I hear Elmer Grady is offering day work breaking sod on another field."

Enoch held out his skinny arms and grinned in spite of his problems. "Can you see a puny feller like me tryin' to break Elmer's sod?" He turned his back. "I'll hafta think of somethin' else," he sighed. "Jus' wanted to let you know, that's all."

Later, as Karl watched Enoch hurry across the field toward home, he reached for the shovel. He couldn't do much, but at least he could share his friend's troubles. And in spite of the grim situation, he'd sent Enoch off with a smile.

Determined not to let things get him down either, he turned back to the barn, and the shoveling that awaited him.

The next morning after milking, Pa sent Stewie to help Karl clean out stalls. Stewie wrinkled his nose in disgust. "I'm sure glad Pa doesn't always make me work in this stuff," he said as he scooped up a shovel of dung.

Karl glared at Stewie. Of all the children in the family, Stewie was the most creative about getting out of anything that smacked of work. Somehow he could tell when Pa had an extra job up his sleeve, then he'd find a piece of harness to mend or a hoe to sharpen and skinny by without any real muscle work. Karl didn't bother to hide his disgust.

"Don't know why you're complaining," he growled. "Ever since I was 6 *I've* been scooping. Why, I've moved enough of this stuff to—"

"Yeah. And that's the difference between intelligence and stupidity," broke in Stewie. "You gotta think fast if you don't want to end out on the wrong end of a shovel till you wrinkle up 'n drop dead."

Karl clamped his mouth shut and dug in. He wanted to use his brain for something more creative too. He wanted to reach out and experience the world and what it had to offer—the places, the sights, the sounds. But he couldn't.

Later that afternoon while Karl mended the corral fence, Pa approached. "I've been thinking on what you said about spring planting—you know, how we should plant corn in the bean field, and beans in the corn patch. I've got to admit it makes sense."

Karl sneaked a look at Pa who up until that very moment had insisted that the idea of rotating crops was pure hogwash. Now he stood, facing the creek field, a thoughtful look on his face.

"Maybe I should listen to you oftener, son. You have some good ideas, but I guess I'm tempted to think I know everything because I've been farming so long."

Karl had waited for a long time to hear words such as Pa had just spoken. But instead of making him feel like a man, a feeling of dread settled over him. Like a heavy quilt it weighed him down, crushing his newest dreams.

Pa scratched his head. "Guess since you're going to own this place someday you should have a pretty heavy say in what we do in the future."

Karl studied the nail he held, then turned to Pa. Hope burned in the man's eyes—the hope of a long and happy relationship with a son who thought farming was the most wonderful thing in the world. How could he disappoint him?

"Y'know, it gives me comfort to realize that even after I'm gone you'll be here keeping this place going. And the family provided for." Pa's forehead bunched up. "Man has only one life to live and it's a little scary knowing you could drop off and leave others in want—just like Schneider did, poor fellow."

Karl didn't like the turn of conversation, though Pa was only saying what the two of them had often discussed when he was younger. But now it seemed like Pa was coiling a rope around his body and slowly cinching it up. That rope was cutting off all chance of real life for Karl.

Pa's beard separated in a smile. "But you'll be here, keeping on, and watching after your ma even after I'm done. Course, I don't plan to be done for a long time."

"But Pa—"

43

Pa held up his hand. "Don't let me keep you from your mending any longer, son." He pointed to Karl's hand. "You sure those nails you're using are long enough?"

Karl nodded. "Pa?"

Pa grinned over his shoulder. "Not now, Karl. Tonight after supper we'll sit down and I'll tell you all my plans for the farm. See what you think of 'em."

What was the use anyway? There was no way out of this kind of life when one was born into it! And Pa just went merrily on thinking Karl's plans were just the same as they had been when he was a little kid tagging along at Pa's heels. With a sigh Karl picked up another nail, positioned it in the board, and sunk it in with four strokes. Then he whacked it once more, just for good measure, leaving a round hole in the board.

Karl stared at the fresh dent. Pa wouldn't like it if he saw that. He'd say it was a sign of a shoddy worker. Karl gritted his teeth and sunk the hammer head into the board again. A splinter chipped away.

What good would it do to share his dreams of something different with Pa? Pa would never listen to how he felt about staying on the farm, and would insist that he take it over, just like he himself had done 20 years before. He whacked the board again, and heard the foot-long split jump down its center. Karl would stay here forever, a slave to the land, a prisoner of his family, with no life of his own. He'd be at the mercy of his lazy brothers and primping sister. Ma would hang on to him, too. There was nothing a fellow could do about it.

When he heard the gate click closed behind him, guilt washed over Karl like a kettle of water sloshing over his head. In a moment Pa would notice the kind of work he'd done, splitting the board and all. And he'd know something was wrong. But Enoch's voice reached out to him instead of Pa's.

Karl spun around, surprised to see his friend again so soon. At least Enoch understood how Karl felt about the farm. Karl's greeting died in his throat as he noticed Enoch's drooping shoulders and long face.

"Thought you'd be in church," Karl blurted. "What's wrong?"

Enoch shrugged. "Went to see 'bout sod breaking. Elmer Grady jus' laughed at me an' said I was too skinny for that kinda work. Said to go home 'n take care of my own place." Enoch wagged his head. "I asked 'round this morning after the preachin', too." He sighed. "Might as well face facts. There ain't no work 'round these parts for me."

Karl's hammer slid to the ground. "But there's gotta be! Surely—"

"So I talked to Ma. When we was at the b-banker's last week she saw a San Francisco paper. Seems there's work to spare out there."

"San Francisco!"

Enoch blanched. "Yeah. Looks like I'll be headin' that way."

"But your place!"

Enoch's wounded eyes pleaded for a way out. "You think I l-like the idea? I love workin' the land. I like bein' with my family! But you gotta understand. There just ain't no m-money left! If I don't go we'll hafta s-sell out, 'n then where'll we be?"

Karl ambled toward the barn, stopped at it's wide door, and idly picked up the scooping shovel which he'd not yet put away. Why, Enoch was the one who really had troubles. He had no choices at all. No Pa to work beside him, to help share the burdens like Karl had.

For once Karl couldn't think of a thing to say. He knew he couldn't fix things up for Enoch this time.

"When'll you go?"

Enoch gulped, and his voice came out funny. "Tomorrow. C-can't waste no more time."

Karl glared across the corral at smelly old Bertha who

watched him with her soft eyes and slobbered cud juice. As he thought of his and Enoch's situations the old anger boiled up again, knotting his insides. He kicked at a clump of dry manure, skittering it across the corral. Bertha didn't even blink.

He'd had his fill of tails stinging his cheeks when he milked, of cleaning stalls amid endless hordes of flies. He didn't want to face another season of hoeing corn or bucking bales. He couldn't mend another fence! For weeks now his resentment against Pa had seethed just under the surface, resentment because Pa kept saying it was his responsibility as eldest son to stay on the family farm and help support the younger ones! How ironic that his best friend was the one to break free, going to the big city! The clincher was that Enoch didn't even want to go!

Enoch swiped his hand across his upper lip, his eyes filled with apology. "Shucks, I didn't mean t' upset 'cha. J-jist thought I'd come 'round to say g'bye." He stared down at his big feet. "Anyways, I might be back. What if I c-can't find work? Y'know how I am about takin'.''

Karl grinned in spite of himself, just picturing Enoch mustering enough courage to ask a stranger for work. It would never happen.

Karl thumped Enoch's shoulder. "Guess I'll hafta come along! I can help you find work!"

Enoch brightened momentarily, then drooped again. "Yer Pa'd never let you!"

Karl stiffened. "Look, I'm nearly a man now, and it's time I make my own decisions! You know how I feel about farming! If I don't break away, I'll likely be here the rest of my life, and I couldn't abide that! Besides, my brothers are old enough to take on my chores, lazy bums!" He faced his friend with a determined look. "It's all settled. I'm going too! I'll send money home if that's what it takes, just so's I get away from the sight of these stupid cows!"

For the rest of the afternoon Karl rehearsed his speech. After supper, when Pa had finished his second piece of raisin pie and headed toward the kitchen rocker, Karl spoke up. "Pa, we gotta talk."

Pa chuckled. "Right you are. Let's go out on the stoop."

It had been an unusually warm day for January, but now the evening chill made them shiver as Pa settled onto the top step. Karl watched his father scan the farmyard—the barn, and the field that sloped off toward the south. He was a careful farmer, not shoddy like some in the area. He insisted that things be kept neat. At least Karl agreed with that.

"Well, son, what I was thinking was—"

"Pa, may I say something first?" Karl interrupted, not daring to wait too long lest he lose his nerve. "Enoch has'ta go to San Francisco to find work 'cause they're out of money. I want to go with him."

To Karl's surprise, Pa's expression didn't even change. But then, from somewhere deep inside came the sound of stifled laughter.

"Getting itchy feet, huh?" Pa's eyes twinkled. "I remember when I felt the same way—felt tied down."

"Then I can go?"

Pa gazed across the field, and it was easy to see the love of the farm mirrored in his eyes. Then his smile faded. "You can't leave, son. We've added the grove, and there's so much that needs to be done. If we plan together carefully, I think we can make good money this year, and then we can—"

"But Pa! I—"

Pa's eyes climbed to Karl's face. His expression still hadn't changed, but his voice was firm. "I need you right here on the farm."

Karl could hold back no longer! He was tired of being taken for granted! It wasn't fair that his life had been mapped out for him as though he had no brain to think for himself! Harsh words bunched up in his mouth, then tumbled out.

"But Pa, I hate farming! Doesn't it matter what I want for my own life?"

Pa arose slowly, and for the first time Karl noticed a stoop to his shoulders. "But the family—we need you to help us keep going—keep ahead."

Karl was livid. "It isn't my fault the family is so big! Why should I have to give up my life for your children?"

Pa's mouth dropped open, and at the same time his face closed. He turned his back and was quiet for a long time. Finally he heaved a sigh. "So you're wanting to head for the big city. You know how dangerous that place can be?"

The quivery feeling inside Karl burst into laughter. No one would ever bother a big fellow like himself, not when he looked so much older than he was. "Enoch's going too, you know. We'll watch out for each other. He needs money for his family and I can send money home too. There's no reason Ralph and Stewie can't take over my chores."

Pa faced him again, and suddenly they were strangers. All was deadly silent except for the pigeon's endless cooing inside the barn. Karl glanced away. He didn't like it when Pa looked like that, so disappointed that his face might crumble. In times past it had always made Karl give in. But it wouldn't this time! He'd made up his mind.

"I see your mind's set, boy," Pa whispered. "It's not your money I want. I don't want you to leave. Not just because you help with this big family, but because I like having my son around." His voice broke, and suddenly Karl realized Pa wasn't as strong as he'd always thought.

Pa fought for control. "But I guess you're right. Times are changing, and I suppose it's fitting you should try your wings." Pa swiped at his nose with the back of his hand. "Just remember, you're always welcome to come home. Your Ma and me, we love you, boy."

Two days later Karl and Enoch shouldered their packs and with only a few dollars between them trudged westward on the dusty road to San Francisco. All the last-minute words of warning and advice Karl had expected from Pa were strangely absent, replaced by wishes for success. As they crossed the last of the Johnson farmland, Karl tried to forget the hurt in Pa's eyes and the tears he'd seen on Ma's cheeks. He shoved aside the memories each landmark stirred. Instead he thought about the adventure that lay ahead—a trek into new places with no one to tell him what to do, the excitement of a big city.

When they topped the rise in the road, Karl eyed the little town that had been the hub of his life. He concentrated on the buildings they passed. He saw the stores and the proud flag that he'd helped hang in front of the schoolhouse during the New Year's Day ceremony a month before. Now there'd be no more school for him. Maybe he'd miss those good times.

Quieter than usual, Enoch trudged along beside Karl in the last boots his Pa had made. Karl watched him from the corner of his eye as the minutes ticked by. Enoch's reluctant steps gradually slowed, and he repeatedly licked his lips like he always did when he was worried and mulling things over.

What if Enoch changed his mind and decided to turn back? After all, he wasn't very adventurous and didn't really want to leave. Maybe he'd change his mind and try again to find work nearby.

Karl's dream of escaping the farm started to weaken. But then he pulled himself up short. Hadn't he always been able to talk Enoch into things? Enoch claimed Karl had a "silver tongue," so if he said the right words he could keep Enoch on the road to 'Frisco.

At last Enoch's pack slid to the tangle of dry weeds beside the road. "I feel so t-twisted up!" he said, shaking his head. "What should I do, anyways?" His eyes brimmed with tears. "Ma needs me at home to k-keep the farm up, but I can't make no cash there." He shoved his hands into his pockets and began to pace. "I gotta go where I can earn m-money, else we'll hafta keep sellin' off th' land. 'Fore long Ma 'n the g-girls won't even have a roof over their heads."

He turned to Karl. "But what if I can't find a job?" His shoulders drooped. "Shucks, what Elmer Grady said the other d-day keeps runnin' round inside my head. I know I don't look strong, even though I am. What'll I do?" Enoch stared longingly back down the road.

Karl thought fast. He had to put some courage into Enoch. It was now or never.

"In a city the size of 'Frisco there's lots of work that doesn't need muscle strength. Remember what Mr. Felder said in class last year? About messengers on bikes and office jobs and all sorts of things? You're quick thinking. You could do a lot of things."

"But I don't talk so good."

"Ah, that don't make no difference!" Karl answered, lapsing into Enoch's version of English. "Besides, I'll help you find somethin' good—just you wait and see. World hasn't beat the two of us yet, 'n it never will!"

Karl smiled to himself as Enoch's uncertainty dropped away. Finally he reached for his pack. "I plumb fergot. Pa'd be disappointed in me, for sure. Why, I just gotta rely on God to help me get the work I n-need so's I can take care of the family. Bible says He will!''

Karl groaned. If Enoch was going to the city to do the work of a man it was time for him to give up his childish attachment to God. "Seems like it'd be smarter to rely on your own wits than on any help from that God of yours," he pointed out. "Doesn't seem like He did much to help your Pa when he was sick, nor any of you since."

Enoch smiled patiently. "That's where yer wrong, Karl," he answered gently. "God helps everyone, but some people are too uppity to realize it." He adjusted the pack on his back and started west again. "God's helped us a'plenty, and someday when you lose that big head of yers, you'll see He's been helpin' you too!"

Karl laughed right out loud as he fell into step with Enoch. If anyone needed help, it surely wasn't him—big and brawny and blessed with a silver-tongue!

The sun had already dipped behind the trees when the two boys pushed through a willow thicket that hugged the edges of a roadside stream. Karl dropped his pack onto the sandy ground and flopped down beside it. "Guess this is as good as any place to sleep. Are my feet tired!"

Enoch sat down beside him and unlaced his heavy boots. Karl watched as he removed a sock and rubbed a red place on his heel. "Shucks, we musta walked 20 miles today. I'm starved!"

Karl opened his pack. They would share the rest of the rolls and cheese their mothers had sent along. Cold water sucked up from the stream completed their scanty fare. Though the sun had not disappeared on the western horizon, as soon as they'd eaten Karl rolled up in his blankets, turning and twisting until he found a comfortable spot. Behind him the creek gurgled on, a restful melody for a weary boy.

"Y'know what I think we should do?" he mumbled, turning over again. But Enoch did not hear for he had gone down the creek and was kneeling in the sand!

Karl watched for a moment, then rolled back over. That religion stuff was the only thing he didn't like about Enoch. It was plain disgusting to see an intelligent person bowing to Someone that wasn't even there! Once at their destination he'd surely realize that his parents had been mistaken about God!

Karl's thoughts turned to the exciting city Mr. Felder had described. He grinned to himself. 'Frisco would soon welcome a smart young fellow who would make his mark! He basked in his golden dream, then dozed off.

Each day the boys walked from sunup until dusk, sleeping in thickets or barns along the way. Once a homeward-bound merchant gave them a lift in his empty wagon. A migrant family picked them up too, but the children were so quarrelsome that Karl make excuses to end the ride much sooner than necessary.

Several days later, footsore and empty-stomached, the two boys stood against the ferry railing, watching their new home draw closer. Even from the middle of the bay the city looked enormous. All Mr. Felder had said could not prepare Karl for the wonderful sight of hundreds of buildings bunched together and spilling down the steep hills to the water's edge.

Karl's heart beat a steady tattoo as he scanned the scene through the tangy salt spray. Somewhere in that maze of streets was their new home and new jobs that would bring them freedom from farm work! Eager to share his excitement, Karl turned to Enoch. But poor Enoch wore such a wistful look that he didn't say a word. Enoch was staring, not toward their future, but back at the shore they had just left behind. Again Karl had misgivings about what he'd taken on. Not only must he find a job for himself, but he'd have to run interference for Enoch, too. And cope with his friend's homesickness. It was a big order.

At last the ferryboat docked and the passengers surged up

the gangplank. Everyone seemed to know where to go, and the boys were swept into the terminal along with the sea of travelers. Then Karl spotted the information desk across the high-ceilinged room. As he led the way through the crowd Karl greeted each person he passed, but no one acted as though he existed. Feeling very out of place, he approached the information desk.

"Excuse me, sir. Where can we find a room to rent?"

The sharp-faced man eyed the boys, then turned to a map on the wall. "These two streets are the best places to find rooming houses." His gaze fastened on their packs. "Will you need help with your trunks?"

"No thank you, sir. We can manage."

The man's eyes narrowed. "Left in a hurry, did you?" He jotted something down, then gave directions to a particular street.

As they headed up a long hill the city pressed in around them, big, noisy, and filled with unfriendly people who paid little attention to them. Karl's stomach growled. They hadn't eaten all day, nor dared they spend a penny of their precious money on the crusty biscuits sold on the street corners they passed. They had no idea how much their lodging would cost.

At last they came to a street lined with rooming houses. Eagerly the two boys scanned the windows for "To Let" signs. At last, near the top of the second hill, Karl spied one hanging on a door. He gave the whitewashed place a quick once-over, noticing the clean, starched curtains in the big downstairs window. He knew Ma would approve of this place.

Karl climbed the short flight of steps and rapped on the door. Shy Enoch hung back.

A woman's head poked out. "Yes?"

Karl stepped forward. "We need a room, please."

The woman wrinkled her nose, as though she smelled something bad. "Don't have any room."

"But your sign—"

"Oh!" she laughed nervously, snatching at the sign. "I'm terribly sorry! I forgot to take it down!"

Karl thanked the woman and rejoined Enoch. "Too bad. It looked like a good place, but there's bound to be more places around here." He had so hoped to get settled quickly—in time for supper, at least. He glanced back at the house. A flutter at the doorway caught his eye as the woman replaced the sign!

"Of all the nerve!" he exploded, halting abruptly. "Look at that!"

Enoch turned and gaped at the sign. "But she said there wasn't no room left."

Karl's pack slid to the ground as the hair on the back of his neck bristled. No one was going to treat them like that, not when he had anything to say about it! "Wait here. I have something to say to that woman!"

Enoch grabbed Karl's sleeve. "No use. Place prob'ly c-costs too much, anyways. Let's j-just go on."

Karl couldn't help noticing Enoch's paleness, nor the way he hunched as he stood there, waiting. The rough bay waters had left him nauseated. He needed a place to lie down, that was for sure. Making trouble wouldn't change things.

Karl swallowed his anger, then he picked up his pack and followed his friend on up the hill. He watched Enoch's run-down heels rise and fall. *Guess we don't look too prosperous,* he thought, *but she could of told the truth.*

He sighed as he plunked one foot in front of the other, and the sound of his heart thudded in his ears. It was already mid-afternoon, and the steep hills blocked out any warmth the sun could give. He glanced at the neat row of whitewashed houses. Would everyone in the city welcome them with the same indifference that the information man and the rooming house woman had? What if they couldn't find a place to stay before nightfall? Where would they sleep? In an alley? By the wharf? An awful thought nibbled at the edges of his mind. *Were his dreams of a good life in the city truly as foolish as his father thought?*

Two hours later the boys trailed a roundish woman up three flights of narrow stairs in the sixth rooming house they'd visited. The landlady in each of the places had eyed the road-dirty boys, clearly reluctant to take them in. Now Mrs. Bidley stopped mid-stair and peered at the boys again. A frown pinched her face as a torrent of words poured from her downturned mouth. "Young fellas come to San Francisco to work all the time. They stay a few days and then leave owing me. You that kind?"

Karl blinked in surprise. "No ma'am, Mrs. Bidley!"

Mrs. Bidley sniffed and continued her journey. At the top of the stairs she opened the first door. "It ain't fancy, but it's clean," she said, her ferret-like eyes piercing through them. "And I like it kept that way. Ain't eager to have no vermin in my woodwork! Now," she wagged a finger at them, "there's no young ladies allowed in your room, quiet is expected at all times—on account of day sleepers, you know—and supper's at six sharp." She plunked her hands on her heavy hips. "You plan to stay, you pay your room and board in advance every Saturday night. No pay, and you're out."

For once Karl did not argue. Though Mrs. Bidley didn't seem kindly, who could tell if they'd find a better place before nightfall? Karl dug their precious dollars from his pocket and dropped most of them into Mrs. Bidley's outstretched hand. She pocketed them without a smile.

"If you boys are expecting anything to eat tonight, you'd better wash up and make it snappy. Don't want you looking like ruffians at my table." She turned to go. "There's water in the basin at the end of the hall. Towel's on the rack."

"Thank you, ma'am," breathed Enoch as they stepped into their attic room. Enoch sagged onto the nearest cot and closed his eyes, while Karl surveyed their new home—a little cubicle with a slanted ceiling that pointed toward a tiny window which faced the busy street, allowing in only a dribble of light. Against one wall stood a small chest of drawers and an old kitchen table with two chairs. A potbellied stove squatted in the corner. He wished there was coal for a fire to take the chill from the room. Then Enoch might feel better.

Karl dropped his pack into the corner and smiled in spite of everything. This was the beginning of his quest to live his own life. These walls would witness his success, would watch him become his own kind of man.

"Let's wash up," he said as he reached for the door handle.

Enoch groaned.

"C'mon. You'll feel better when you get some hot food into your belly!"

After a quick wash, the boys followed their noses to the dining room and found a dozen men surrounding an enormous table. Karl's stomach growled as he caught sight of a platter of fried chicken passing from man to man, closely followed by potatoes and a bowl of cooked carrots.

At first they stood in the doorway, not knowing exactly what to do next. Friendly banter bounced back and forth between the men as different ones reported on their day.

Then Mrs. Bidley hurried in with another platter heaped with chicken. "C'mon in, you two. Sit at that end. There."

Everyone stopped talking and suddenly Karl felt as self-conscious as Enoch usually acted. The room went silent and all eyes fastened on him.

Mrs. Bidley plunked the platter of chicken onto the table. "These boys are Karl and Enoch, come to make their fortune in the big city. They took the attic room."

The men grunted hello, looked them over for one more uncomfortable second, then returned to their conversations.

Karl led the way to the bench he and Enoch were to share. Immediately the platters of food came their way. As he helped himself and passed the food on he noticed that Enoch looked totally miserable. Karl was uneasy too, but there was no way he'd ever show it! People tended to take advantage of fellows who were timid and he didn't want to give anyone that chance. He figured that in time they'd both get used to the newness.

A few minutes later a tall, well-dressed gentleman sauntered through the door and settled into the only empty place. "Howdy, friends," he quipped with an air of easy belonging. "Had a good day?"

This time the men didn't just nod and grunt, but each responded with some pleasant remark. It was evident by their actions that even though he couldn't be more than 20, this person was highly thought of by the other boarders.

The fellow glanced around the table. "New boarders, Mrs. Bidley?" he asked.

The woman hurried to his side with the chicken. "Yes, sir, Mr. Polson."

He flashed a warm smile at the boys. "They've been on the road a spell, I'll wager. Make sure you fill 'em up."

Mrs. Bidley warmed. "I'm already doing that, Mr. Polson. Those boys do look like they need fattening." She glowed at Enoch. "Did you get some of everything, lad?"

Enoch flushed. "Y-Yes'm."

"Well, eat up, then. There's plenty more when that's gone."

"What are you fellows aiming to do in our city?" asked Mr. Polson.

Karl put down his fork. "Find work."

Mrs. Bidley slid a plate of biscuits in front of the young man. "Mr. Polson here, he came to the city three years ago, did so well he already owns his own company." She looked as proud as though she'd accomplished the feat herself.

Mr. Polson tossed her a smile. "A team and wagon, that is," he laughed. "Name's Zachary, fellows. I keep telling her to call me that. And don't listen to any of Mrs. Bidley's bragging about my accomplishments. It was just luck, that's all."

Karl relaxed, glad that in the crush of older men they'd found one young and friendly soul. With a boarder like Zachary Polson, this place wouldn't be so bad. And if young Zachary could make good in the city, Karl saw no reason he couldn't do it, too.

Dinner had hardly finished before Mrs. Bidley shooed everyone away from the table so the kitchen girl could clean up. Even though Enoch was still kind of droopy Karl felt too keyed up to settle down yet.

"Let's go take a look around," he urged, prodding Enoch along. Enthused with everything he saw, he wanted Enoch to feel that way, too. But Enoch looked as though thoughts of home still tormented him. Karl knew he must turn his friend's mind to something else—and soon.

"She's sort of feisty, that Mrs. Bidley," he said. Enoch nodded as they headed down the block. "But she sort of warmed up there at the end, did you notice? Maybe she'll be nicer when she gets to know we're honest fellows."

Enoch hunched into himself, looking more miserable than ever. Karl shook his head. Unless his friend quit acting so forlorn no one would hire him. Employers looked for brawny, outgoing people, not timid weaklings. But then Karl remembered all Enoch had been through in the last few months, with his Pa dying and all. He'd willingly accepted the heavy responsibilities of providing for the family, now that his father was gone. Karl knew he was worrying about how his mother would manage all the chores herself and the money she already needed. Karl's heart softened. He mustn't be too harsh in his judgments.

Karl's thoughts continued as they walked. What if Enoch couldn't find a job right away? It wouldn't matter between them. Silently he vowed to take care of everything, to keep Enoch from suffering any more than he had to. After all, what were best friends for?

They turned another corner and headed down a steep street. "Hey, Enoch, if we don't like it at Mrs. Bidley's, we can move to a better place later. We'll get work tomorrow."

Enoch smiled for the first time in an hour. "I pray you're right."

Karl rolled his eyes. Enoch was always praying about something, and it only weakened him. He'd have to make some changes to survive. Karl felt sure of that.

The next morning Enoch found a job as stock boy in a department store a few blocks away, "I reckon God showed me right where t' go. There was a sign right in the window," he prattled happily as they sprawled in their room after dark. "Y' know how flustered 'n tongue-tied I get 'round strangers, 'n Mr. Belkenstein's the first man I asked."

Karl choked back an irritated laugh. Imagine being silly enough to think God had something to do with a fellow finding a job! That was pure foolishness! It was merely a stroke of luck—being in the right place at the right time. But Karl kept his thoughts to himself, glad that for the moment Enoch was happy again.

"Well, I'll look again tomorrow," Karl said confidently. "I won't jump at the first position I'm offered, y'know. I want to find just the right thing. But tomorrow's the big day. I can feel it in my bones."

However, when Saturday night rolled around and it was time to pay the weekly rent again, Karl stood down the hall by the wash basin and stared at himself in the mirror. He was big and strong and handsome in his own way, and up until this time he'd been real sure that he could make a go of it in the world. But, surprisingly enough, he still had no job. In fact, he hadn't had a hint of an offer.

His hazel eyes stared back at him from the cracked mirror, narrow and accusing. *What's wrong with me anyway? I look older than I am and jolly people up. I even look responsible. There's not a job around I couldn't do if I put my mind to it.*

He heaved a sigh and raked his comb through his tangle of dark, wavy hair. What if he didn't find work in the coming week and Enoch had to take care of him with some of his hard-earned money? The very thought twisted Karl's insides. He tried to look confident, unconcerned, but it was getting harder.

"Maybe we should pray about yer gettin' a job," blurted Enoch a few minutes later as he dropped his overalls over the back of the chair.

That did it! Karl was tired of Enoch always talking about his God as though He were Someone who really cared! In a flash of anger he smacked his fist into his other hand. "I wish you'd quit talking such nonsense," he hissed, his voice rising in spite of Mrs. Bidley's noise rule. "You know good and well God doesn't fix things for people, if there is such a thing as God. A man's gotta make his own way, not cling to foolish notions." The words bubbled out, unchecked. "If you wanta believe that stuff I can't stop you, but don't mention God to me again!"

Their neighbor thudded something against their wall and brought Karl up short.

"You hear?" he finished in an angry whisper. Enoch dropped onto his cot and pulled the heavy quilt over himself. He plumped his pillow once or twice, then sighed deeply. "I hear, b-but I ain't m-making no promises."

Day after hopeless day passed as Karl trudged the streets, looking for work. No one seemed to need him. Each night at supper Zachary and the other men around the table asked if he'd found work. Night after night he watched them raise their eyebrows when he had to admit the truth. Karl was coming to the point where he seriously considered skipping supper, it was so hard to face up to those men and their knowing smiles.

"Not everyone has young Zachary's luck," Harry Wimbley said one night, his doughy jowls quivering as he sat in judgment across the table. "But you shoulda found something by now!"

Karl put on his bravest front. "I want just the right position, Mr. Wimbley. Not just any job."

Karl couldn't miss the men's reactions. Determined not to show his feelings, he stuffed a bite of turnip into his mouth. He envied the way the others treated Zachary—like he was a step above, or something. Zachary let the compliments fall where they would. His air of easy success affected everyone, demanding their respect.

Karl wished he could be like Zachary.

The next Saturday night when Enoch dug more money from his pocket to pay Mrs. Bidley for their room, Karl's courage collapsed. Who would have thought that Enoch would end up supporting him? Each day without work became harder to face. It was impossible to pretend that everything would turn out all right any more.

That evening the boys ambled down to the wharf just to get out of their room for awhile. Karl broke into Enoch's chatters "Guess I'll head back home," he sighed as he gazed toward the lights on the far shore.

Enoch flung a pebble into the bay. "If you weren't so stubborn you'd already have a job."

Karl flared. "I've tried everything, and you know it!" He

spun around and faced his puny friend. "I've answered every ad I could, and asked in all sorts of places. Fate's just against me, that's all."

Enoch became wary. "You ain't p-prayed about it." Karl swallowed the angry words that threatened to explode from him. Enoch had been so generous throughout the past few weeks, never pointing out his friend's failures. How dare he lash out at him just because he truly believed in God. That was the way he'd been taught. Besides, he'd tried before and learned there was no use reasoning with Enoch when it came to religion.

"If you want to pray so bad, go ahead," Karl blurted. Oblivious to people who might see him, Enoch knelt and prayed right there on the wharf. And the next afternoon Karl landed a job driving a wagon for a produce merchant!

After work that first night Karl studied Enoch with renewed interest. Who was this God that Enoch spoke to? Who made changes for him? Maybe religion wasn't just for trembly old ladies after all. Karl had never gone to church, but now his interest had been sparked. He prided himself on being a progressive young man—one that knew how to take advantage of opportunities such as Enoch's God seemed to present. And so he determined that the next time Enoch went to church, he'd go along too.

After all, the way to success was often by strange routes, and one thing he had already determined, he was going to be successful. Just like Zachary Polson.

$\mathbf{A}$ few weeks later the damp hand of predawn fog wrapped around Karl as he climbed into the high wagon and flicked the reins. Soon the four-horse team he drove for Mr. Tweedy leaned into the harness and the heavy load began to move along the waterfront toward the ferry building.

Somewhere in the distance a dog yapped, then quieted. The team's clopping footfalls echoed against the warehouses as they passed, a ringing sound in the early morning. Karl sucked in a deep breath. He liked the salty tang that blew in from the bay. The moist air was tinged now and again with a hint of the fish that were even then being unloaded from fishing vessels. Few people were out yet, and he savored this peaceful time as his favorite part of the day.

Though he sometimes missed the quietness of his old home, Karl loved the city and its moods and again felt the thrill of being a part of the modern world. How often his parents had spoken of the evils of the city, as though scoundrels lurked around every corner. He smiled to himself. If only they could see 'Frisco as she really was! He supposed there was evil to be found, but it just depended on where a fellow looked.

When his stomach rumbled he reached into his pocket for the bulging napkin he'd tucked there the night before. Because he left the boarding house so early in the morning he didn't have the luxury of a good breakfast. Tanny, the kitchen girl, must have noticed for each evening she waited until sharp-eyed Mrs. Bidley looked the other way before she tucked a couple dinner rolls under her apron and later wrapped them in a napkin. With a shy smile, she'd slip them to Karl. "For tomorrow," she'd whisper. She was a very nice girl.

Now the crusty rolls stilled his gnawing stomach, and by the time he turned the team onto Market Street a little morning light seeped through the fog blanketing the city. At the flick of the reins, Jacob, the lead horse, snorted a white plume of breath and threw his whole weight into the harness. The other horses followed his example, and with a groan they began the long uphill pull.

Here there were more people on the street—owners sweeping their front walks, maids hurrying to begin their daily chores, and two furtive young boys with packs on their backs. Ahead, another drayman unloaded crates and plunked them onto the street. Karl smiled, thinking of the first few weeks he and Enoch had been in San Francisco. At first they had doubted the wisdom of staying in the noisy city with its strange smells and unfriendly people. But once they had become accustomed to its bustling, and to Mrs. Bidley and her bossy ways, and once they had accepted the fact that no one else could be expected to cook like their own mothers, they settled down happily enough.

True to his decision, Karl had gone to church with Enoch on the first Sunday after finding his job as a drayman. He looked over the congregation in surprise, for he saw as many men as women, and not old men, either. Instead they were young successful-looking types who seemed as normal and outgoing as anyone he'd ever met.

Karl listened to the preacher with a growing sense of awe, for the man didn't expound on the fires of hell and how each one sitting there was headed that way, as he'd expected from what

Pa had always told him. Instead, the black-robed preacher spoke of a Jesus that really loved sinners. He said it mattered to Jesus when life was hard, or disappointments were many. He told how this Jesus helped men and women change habits that caused them problems. By merely accepting this man, Jesus, one could be saved and look forward to an eternity in heaven where life would always be pleasant.

Though Karl could not quite swallow everything the pleasant-faced preacher had told them, he was favorably impressed, and when Enoch slipped to his knees for his bedtime prayer that Sunday, Karl did too—though only for a brief instant, for he felt shy about letting Enoch witness his change of behavior.

When at last the wagon crested the hill Karl's thoughts returned to the present, and he guided the panting team to the edge of the road for a moment's rest. Then they continued their journey, picking up speed until a whitewashed store with counters along the front loomed beside them. Karl pulled to the curb, vaulted the sideboard, and fastened the leather strap to the hitching post. Then he began unloading, placing boxes of vegetables and fruits just where fussy Mr. Steinert insisted they must be.

By then it was light, and housewives and kitchen maids scurried about with baskets in their arms, pinching oranges and sniffing potatoes, eager to make their purchases for the day. Mr. Steinert was upon him immediately, glaring from deep-set eyes.

"You're late again, boy!" he bellowed in his mixed-up accents "From deese ladies I von't make any money eef Bernheim's receives hes vegetables before me. You know good vives likes to shop early!"

Karl nodded. "Shipment came in late, sir. I'll try not to let it happen again."

Mr. Steinert snorted as Karl turned back to his task. Funny, but just a few weeks earlier Karl would have lashed right back at the crabby businessman, even if it had lost him his job. But the preacher's words about God helping people to control themselves had stuck with him. Only half-believing at first, he had silently asked God to help him hold his tongue, and He had. To Karl's surprise, his fiery temper didn't get the best of him nearly as often.

When Karl had finished his early-morning deliveries he headed back down Market Street. Now the avenues were crowded with wagons and buggies. The early-morning mist had lifted, and from the top of the hill he could look down upon the Ferry Building with its big clock tower. Just beside it in the bay, a ferry bobbed—loading, he supposed—for its journey across the water to Oakland. The ornate black hands on the clock tower pointed to 10 minutes after eight. It was past time for him to be back to the waterfront for his next load.

Just as he flicked the reins a wagon pulled alongside. "Ha! Karl! How's it going?" called Zachary who perched in his shiny red wagon. The ornate black letters, "Polson's Deliveries," stood out in sharp contrast along its side. A mound of fine trunks, carefully padded and strapped to keep them from shifting on the steep hills, lay in the wagon bed.

"I'm heading for the Ferry," Zachary announced, eyeing the bed of Karl's wagon. Bits of lettuce and wilted carrots were littered across it. The young man grinned. "This is a heap more pleasant than hauling food. It never rots."

Envy threatened Karl. How long would it be before he would be as well off as Zachary? True, he liked working for Mr. Tweedy, but how much nicer it would be to be his own boss—to dress like Zachary, to have the men at the boardinghouse look up to him, to drive a fine wagon.

Perhaps Zachary read Karl's thoughts for he turned to the boy and said, "It all takes time, my friend. Meanwhile, how'd you like to work for me?"

A shiver climbed Karl's spine. "What do you say?"

Zachary said with a grin. "I'm getting another rig pretty soon. Just waiting to close the deal. And of course I can't drive two wagons at once!"

Karl thought of kind Mr. Tweedy, a wiry little man with garlic breath and a twitchy moustache, who had hired him to drive for Tweedy's Fine Produce. The man had gone out of his way to help Karl, giving him advantages that one would usually save for a son. Would it be fair for him to quit driving for Mr. Tweedy just when he had learned his route? A pang of loyalty threatened him. But he pushed it aside.

A fellow had to think of himself first if he planned to get ahead in the world. He considered the woolen sock he kept hidden under his mattress—the money sock that had belonged to Grandpap. Ma had tucked it into his pack for good luck, last thing. Each week after paying his board and room he shoved as much money as he could into it, saving for his own team and wagon. If he was careful he could save as much as two dollars a week. That was a lot. But if he worked for Zachary, he'd rub shoulders with the city's rich people. He'd become well known. That could be an advantage.

Before Karl had a chance to ask questions, a wagon pulled up behind them. "Move on!" the driver bellowed.

Zachary shrugged. "We'll talk about it later," he called as he flicked his reins.

That night after their usual game of checkers, and after Karl had blown out the lamp and slipped between his sheets, he told Enoch what Zachary had said. "When I saw him after supper he told me that he'd pay me fifty cents more a day to drive for him. I could save three extra dollars a week! Zachary'll have the new rig next month."

For a moment Karl thought that Enoch had fallen asleep, for there was no answer. He sighed and visualized himself smartly dressed, driving a shiny red Polson's wagon, hauling luggage or dry goods for merchants, rather than vegetables and crates of squawking chickens. He wondered what his father would think of him, all slicked up like a city gent rather than wearing farm overalls. He would certainly have to agree that Karl had chosen wisely when he decided to go to the city. And then there was Tanny. He grinned into the darkness.

"I d-don't think you should do it," Enoch blurted.

Karl flinched. "Why not?"

"That Zachary, he don't s-seem honest somehow. I jus' don't trust 'im." Enoch's bed squeaked as he flopped over. "There's somethin' fishy 'bout him, 'specially such b-big talk 'bout high wages."

Karl's heels plunked onto the cold wooden floor as he sat right up. "Don't be ridiculous! Can't you see, if I work for Zachary I'll be able to buy my own rig sooner. I came to the city to make it big. Why should I waste my time in a lower-paying job?"

Karl could hear Enoch scratching. "Money's not everything," he said a moment later. " 'Sides, Mr. Tweedy's been right g-good to you 'n he's gettin' on in years. Wouldn't s'prize me none if he up and made you his p-partner someday."

Karl mulled that over. Mr. Tweedy did seem partial to him—favoring him over those who had worked for him for several years. And he really was fond of the man. Relieved that he needn't make up his mind about the matter quite yet, Karl settled back under his quilts. There was plenty of time left before Zachary's deal would close.

As the boys talked on, Enoch hesitantly made an announcement of his own. His wage had been raised to 19 cents an hour, so he would be able to send even more money home. That was all good and well, but with spring coming on he hadn't been able to put the farmwork out of his mind, and Ma wasn't all that strong.

"Th' idea's been buzzin' around in my head fer a l-long time, and I reckon I'd better be headin' back home so's I kin manage the summer work. After harvest I'll come back. M' boss sez he'll save my job.''

Enoch's startling idea hovered in the darkness until Karl exploded. "That's the dumbest thing I've ever heard, after getting such a good raise!''

Enoch sighed. "Kinda figgered that's how you'd feel. Don't look like neither of us thinks m-much of the other feller's idea, but we both gotta do what seems best to our'sels. Everything works together for good to them that loves the Lord, I always say.''

"I know you do,'' Karl grumbled, unable to count the times Enoch had murmured those same few words just since they'd come to 'Frisco. In spite of his dawning awareness of God, Karl got a little tired of hearing it! Then he sobered. Sometimes Enoch was a pain, but how would things seem without him around?

The night chill clamped its hand over their little room as Karl pondered the quick turn of events. It hadn't been hard to figure that Enoch didn't like Zachary. Truth was, he hadn't warmed up to him one bit. Though he hadn't been unpleasant, Enoch just melted into the woodwork when Zachary came around. It might even be a relief if Enoch did go home. Lately they didn't think alike about several things.

Karl listened as Enoch's breathing evened out and sleep claimed him. Enoch always dropped off fast. He'd give that slow smile and say that it was because God did his worrying. Well, he—Karl—would handle his own!

Then a terrible thought jolted Karl! If he couldn't split the rent with Enoch he couldn't tuck as much money into Grandpap's sock! That meant he wouldn't be able to get his own rig as soon as he'd hoped! He lay in frozen silence for a few minutes, pondering his problem. Surely there were plenty of fellows wandering around town that would be glad for a roommate. Maybe even Zachary would consider doubling up!

Karl stared into the darkness as he mulled over what lay ahead. He had vowed he'd never work the land again, and he meant it! Now he had a chance to step up. It just made good sense to accept Zachary's offer. With hard work and planning and the respect he'd surely earn, someday he'd be rich. Maybe Enoch would just have to go his own way.

He turned his back to the tiny square of light the window made and let pleasant thoughts fill his mind. In spite of Enoch or anyone else life was going to be wonderful.

CHAPTER

It had been a week since Enoch had announced his plans to go home come summertime, and still Zachary hadn't said a word about Karl working for him once he got the new rig. Suppertime came and went each evening without the tiniest hint that Zachary even remembered the conversation. Karl had begun hanging around after dinner just in case he might mention it. But as the meal ended evening after evening and Zachary went off to do whatever it was he did after supper, Karl's hope sagged a little further. He had begun to count on earning a lot more money. By the end of Zachary's fifth evening of silence an uncomfortable thought nagged Karl. Maybe Zachary had been making idle conversation that day when he'd dangled the new job before him like a rabbit before a hound's nose. Foolishly, he'd jumped at the bait.

With the hope of working for Zachary dwindling, the only good thing about going to supper other than to fill his empty stomach was the chance to see Tanny again. It was clear that the kitchen girl noticed him—not just because she slipped him rolls each evening, but because of the way she acted. She wasn't bold enough to come right out and speak, but she did keep an eye on things and made sure Karl's plate didn't get empty before the great bowls of food headed his way again. And his pie always seemed a little larger than the pieces he saw on the other men's plates.

In spite of his disappointment, Karl smiled to himself. Why, any time he felt like it he could conjure up her image in his mind. She was slender, almost too tiny to carry the big trays that Mrs. Bidley filled, and long brown hair framed her pale, oval face. He liked her shy smile, the way she dropped her eyes, and how the pink seeped into her cheeks when she caught him watching her. Karl went all soft inside. If he had his own rig, then maybe . . .

Karl reined in his thoughts. There would be no girls for him for a long, long time. If he ever did get married, he didn't want his wife to work hard like Ma did, getting old before her time. His wife would have a city house and would take care of their own family—not hire out for the day. But Zachary's silence caused Karl's dreams to fade into nothingness, destroying his hope of financial independence for years to come.

Seven days after they'd talked, Karl sagged against the wall on the way to supper, hardly able to face the group again. "I'm so tired tonight," he moaned.

Enoch eyed him. "Ain't no wonder. Every night I hear ya' tossin' around, winding yerself up in yer bed covers."

"Think I'll tuck in right after supper. Mind if we skip checkers tonight?"

Enoch chuckled. "Prob'ly be the turnin' point of my whole life and things'll go downhill ever after."

For once Zachary was already in his place when Karl and Enoch entered the dining room. Karl tried to ignore Zachary, not wanting him to think he'd been gullible enough to take their earlier conversation serious.

After downing several helpings of roast as well as potatoes and cabbage swimming in butter Karl felt a little better, though unusually tired. Tanny fluttered in and out of the kitchen, her cheeks two bright roses beneath gentle eyes. She'd been at the beck and call of Mrs. Bidley all day. She must be tired, too.

Zachary kept the other men laughing that evening, relating an experience he'd had with a crochety old couple and their rat-sized white dog. Then, as everyone left the supper table, Zachary beckoned to Karl.

"I'm heading out to look at that rig I told you about. Why not come along to see what you think of it?"

So Zachary hadn't been joking after all! Karl's weariness vanished and the dreams he'd built rushed back into place. There really would be more money!

Karl could hardly wait to go! Then he remembered the game of checkers he had canceled due to tiredness. He watched Enoch walk away. It wouldn't be fair to brush him off after he'd been so nice about their game.

"Mind if Enoch rides along?"

Zachary's eyes narrowed for the briefest moment. Then he slipped his thumbs under his suspenders and grinned. "Why not? See you two out back in about five minutes."

Soon they rode into the brisk evening behind Zachary's sleek pair. Here and there men waved and greeted Zachary. Pride swelled in Karl's chest. Of all those successful people, he'd been singled out to be Zachary's partner!

"How'd you accomplish so much in just three years?" Karl asked, eager to discover Zachary's key to success.

Zachary doffed his hat to a businessman. "It's a long story," he said with a modest chuckle.

Karl glanced at a pretty girl and the older woman who accompanied her as they strolled down the walk. He imagined how lovely Tanny would look dressed in such finery. "Hope I can do as well as you have."

"Just watch your opportunities, friend. Never let one slip past."

Karl grinned at Enoch, but Enoch did not respond. Karl shrugged. Why did Enoch have to be such a wet blanket? Maybe he was just sore about checkers, but he'd changed so much lately. Seemed like there were lots of things Karl wanted to do that made Enoch turn up his nose. Once long ago Pa had told him that it was possible for even best friends to grow apart as they got older and matured. Perhaps that's what was happening to he and Enoch.

Karl discarded the thought and turned his attentions to matters at hand. This was no time to worry. He needed to keep his ears and eyes open, to discover Zachary's tricks of the trade. Then perhaps he'd stumble onto one of those opportunities Zachary had mentioned.

Up and down the hills they drove, into the thinning countryside. When Zachary finally turned onto a dusty lane, a man hurried to meet them. "Just pull around back."

A moment later Zachary beckoned to Karl. "Come take a look at her."

The wagon was in excellent condition, the horses sturdy and bright-eyed. Karl said nothing as he watched Zachary inspect everything, then stand and twist his moustache for awhile.

"Looks like the wagon's been a far piece," Zachary said at last. "You still holding for the same price?"

Mr. Jacobs kicked at a pebble. "Wouldn't sell at all, except the wife's sick and I've got to lay my hands on some quick cash. You know that."

Zachary's sympathetic gaze settled on the older man. "It's all so unfortunate. But maybe I can help you out. What's your best price?"

Mr. Jacobs sagged, then shoved his hands into his pockets before he named a ridiculously low figure.

Karl's stomach lurched! Why, Zachary could turn around and sell the wagon for nearly twice as much! But to Karl's surprise, Zachary didn't respond. Instead he looked the wagon over once again, ran his hand down the horses legs, checked their teeth and hooves, then stepped away,

"Thanks for your time, Jacobs," he said coolly. "We'll be going now."

Mr. Jacobs stiffened, panic in his eyes, "Aren't you interested?"

"Your price is pretty steep for a rig in this condition, don't you think?" Zachary hedged. "I'll have to think it over."

Enoch slunched down in the seat as though trying to make himself invisible, and Karl sat open-mouthed as Zachary cracked the whip and they headed back toward the city.

Amused, Zachary glanced at Karl. "You never take a man's first price, you know. Sometimes not even his second. Time usually changes people's minds about the value of their goods. He'll be calling on me before the week is out, I'll wager."

Karl thought of the poor man's sick wife. He remembered the trapped look on his face. "But that was a good price!" he blurted.

Zachary laughed. "It was very good. But I'm in business, friend—out to get everything I can for my dollar. I can't help what his problems are." He sighed. "You don't make it in the business world by worrying about charity. Just watch. That fellow will come around yet, and at an even more attractive price."

Karl studied Zachary's handsome profile as they passed a lighted corner. He was confident and had a good business head. And everyone he knew looked up to Zachary. *Perhaps one really couldn't be held responsible for another man's trouble,* Karl pondered. *I've just been taught differently, that's all. By farming people. Not by men smart enough to move up in the world.* He frowned and crowded an uneasy twinge from his thoughts.

Later on in their room, Karl faced Enoch, suddenly irritated by his friend's behavior. He stood looking down at him. "You sure were stuffy tonight, " he accused. "What's the matter with you, anyhow?"

Enoch hunched into himself like he always did when they disagreed, It was a moment before he answered. "I j-just don't like Zachary, that's all."

"And why not?" Karl's voice climbed again.

Enoch shrugged. "Can't you s-see he's trying to cheat that p-poor man? A person who'll cheat one man'll cheat the n-next—maybe even you."

Karl stood tall, the way Zachary would have. "How can you say he's cheating, tell me that! Are you a businessman or something? Do you own your own rig? My pa never made it anywhere in the world, and neither did yours! You wanta know why? They didn't have a business head, that's why! And you fault Zachary because he does!"

Enoch fumbled with his shirt buttons. His face had gone pale. "My pa, he was s-successful. Raised up an honest family, he d-did. Was honest and had m-mercy on his n-neighbors." He shook his head miserably, peeled off his shirt, and hung it on a wall hook. Then he faced Karl. "M-makes me sick t' see ya' tryin' to act l-like Zachary."

Karl was indignant. "Who said I'm trying to act like Zachary?"

"Well, l-look at yerself," Enoch answered, unbuttoning his pants. "Yer startin' to t-talk like him, walk like him, an' now even think l-like him. Agree'n it's jist f-fine t' take advantage of a man that's d-down. I declare!"

Fire swept through Karl's veins. He flung his jacket onto the chair. "And what's so bad about trying to change from a country boy into a gentleman?" he yelped, thinking again of Zachary's fine clothes and the way others admired him. "A fellow has a right to advance in this world, that is if he can." He thrust his forefinger at Enoch. "I think you're just jealous that I'm making new friends, and you're afraid you'll get left behind. You always did want to keep me to yourself."

Enoch clutched his suspenders, his mouth hanging open. He

stood there for a long moment, regarding Karl in disbelief. "That ain't t-true and you know it! But that Zachary P-polson ain't a good influence on you. Betcha he'll take advantage of you first chance he g-gits!" He let his pants drop around his ankles and kicked to send them across the room. "Yer Pa'd be right upset if h-he could see you lollygagging after that dandy."

Karl's big hands curled into fists. He didn't want to think about Pa or the country way of doing things. And for once he was too angry to respond to the "holier than thou" upstart whom he had mistaken as his best friend. What right did Enoch have standing in judgment? It would be a dark day at high noon before he'd let Enoch tell him what to do!

A brittle silence fell over the boys for the rest of the evening, and that night when Enoch knelt beside his bed, Karl didn't join him.

The evening after their quarrel Karl didn't wait for Enoch before going to the dining room. For once he arrived before anyone else, and quietly slipped into his place. A moment later Tanny backed through the swinging kitchen door, her small hands clutching a huge bowl. Steam from its contents wafted upward as she headed for the table.

Karl jumped up and took the heavy bowl from her. Surprised, she met his gaze for only a moment before looking away. "Thank you," she whispered as she escaped to the kitchen.

He waited at the door and helped her with the next bowl. The shy smile that played upon her lips tugged at Karl's heart and his mouth went dry. Before he could think of anything to say, Tanny disappeared again.

As the boarders ate that night, it was hard not to notice that Tanny took special care to serve Karl first and with the best. In fact, she kept his milk glass topped so well that Mrs. Bidley's eyebrows finally climbed her forehead, and in her curt way she reminded Tanny that other people might be thirsty too.

Obediently, Tanny circled the table with her frosty pitchers. Only once did she steal a glance at Karl. When their eyes met Karl winked, which made Tanny blush and scurry all the faster. That night while Enoch read, Karl lay on his bed reliving the dining room scenes. It hardly seemed possible that a girl like Tanny could be sweet on him. Much later he drifted off to sleep with that hope enfolding him like a soft, warm blanket.

Each morning after that, Karl hurried down the long dark streets thinking about Tanny. Mr. Tweedy greeted him cheerfully. "Top of the mornin', m'boy!" he called out, rain or shine. "The Lord's given us another fine day!"

As Karl helped to load potatoes, cabbages, oranges and chickens into the wagon and hitched up the team, he and Mr. Tweedy shared dockside news. Sometimes Mr. Tweedy talked about his own family and his wish that he had a son just like Karl.

Karl remembered Enoch's remark about Mr. Tweedy viewing Karl as his own son and as a possible partner in the future. A few weeks before, such a prospect would have delighted him. But now—now his head was filled with dreams of quick wealth and of becoming rich and as important as Zachary.

Worry nibbled at the back of Karl's mind. What would he say if Mr. Tweedy really did offer him a more attractive position? Almost unconsciously he turned any personal conversations away from himself, fearing that he might have to hurt the gentle man's feelings. He had set his eyes upon his goals. He would work for Zachary until he had stuffed enough money into Grandpap's sock to buy his own shiny wagon and he'd have a big "Johnson's" painted in fancy letters on its side. He couldn't chance letting anything sidetrack him from that dream, even if it meant disappointment for friendly Mr. Tweedy.

A few evenings later Karl dawdled over his pie long enough for all the other men to leave the dining room. Mrs. Bidley had gone into the kitchen for something while Tanny stacked dirty dishes from the other end of the huge table onto a kitchen tray. Gathering every bit of courage he could, Karl sucked in his breath and approached Tanny. The top of her head barely reached his shoulder, and their close proximity made his heart pound. "Oh, Tanny—" he began.

Startled by his closeness, she glanced up, and then continued her clearing.

"I was wondering, would you like to go walking Sunday afternoon?" he blurted, his tongue stumbling over the words.

She nearly dropped a cup. "Mother doesn't allow me to walk with gentlemen," she hedged. "She—"

Karl thought fast. "How clumsy of me!" he said. "What I meant to ask was if you and your mother would care to go walking. It would be a pleasure to meet the woman who raised such a fine lass." Tanny's blush tugged at his heart-strings, encouraging him. "May I have the honor of calling for both of you at two on Sunday afternoon?"

Tanny's hands moved feverishly as she filled the tray, but a smile played on her lips. "Yes, I would like that," she finally whispered. Then she scurried into the kitchen, completely forgetting her tray of dishes.

Karl stared after her, watching the swinging door until it stopped. Then he left the dining room and bounded up the stairs, two at a time, to his room. Already his mind was busy, planning for Sunday. After his first deliveries the next morning, he would take some of the money he'd hoarded away in Grandpap's sock and buy a new shirt. He'd polish up his boots, too.

Karl became so engrossed in his thoughts that he scarcely noticed Enoch waiting at their table, the checkers laid out as usual. He grabbed his jacket and headed out the door. It was a nice evening, a perfect time to look at shirts in store windows.

Karl skipped church on Sunday, faking weariness. Instead he lay in bed, dreaming of the afternoon. He felt he'd have to do all the talking. Tanny was so shy that he figured she wouldn't say much. Though chatter came easy for him, Karl feared he'd run out of things to say.

Their walk turned out to be delightful. Karl called for Tanny and her mother at their home, a whitewashed bungalow perched on the side of a nearby hill. After the introductions and some polite small talk with Mrs. Graystone, the trio strolled through the park where they fed the ducks. Even though a gusty wind whipped Tanny's pink dress around her ankles, and both she and her mother had to keep close watch on their hats, the hour in the park passed pleasantly enough.

When they had finished there, Karl turned to Mrs. Graystone. "Would you two ladies like a cup of hot chocolate?"

Mrs. Graystone exchanged glances with Tanny, whose cheeks matched the color of her dress, then nodded. "That would be lovely, Mr. Johnson."

Karl smiled and held out his elbows for both of the ladies, and the three turned toward town. Tanny's hand rested lightly on Karl's arm, and a pleasant fire warmed the spot it touched. He slowed his steps, not so much to make walking easy for his two companions, but to prolong the time of actual contact with the lovely girl who glided along beside him.

At the bottom of the hill The Sweet Shoppe buzzed with Sunday-afternoon strollers. The threesome perched at a small round table, and Karl gleefully ordered big mugs of steaming chocolate and a little plate of tea cakes for them to share. To Karl's delight he found that Mrs. Graystone was a very pleasant woman, not hawkish as he had feared. Better yet, away from Mrs. Bidley's stern gaze, Tanny relaxed considerably, even laughing and entering into the conversation a time or two.

With a promise to call upon the two ladies again, Karl began to daydream about knowing Tanny better. She was such a pleasant girl—slender and frail but strong, too. Too bad she must work so hard for such a shrewish woman, but he couldn't help but be glad that she did. Otherwise he'd never have met her.

10

As the days passed, suppertime took on an added glow for Karl. Suddenly the need for food paled in comparison to his desire to see Tanny. Often he found her watching him as she bustled about, keeping the bowls and platters filled. Once or twice Mrs. Bidley sharply reminded her of her duties. Then Tanny's cheeks flamed, and she would duck her head, hurrying even faster.

One evening Karl again dawdled after supper until the other boarders left. Mrs. Bidley was in the kitchen and Tanny had just come back into the room to clear the table.

"I need to talk to you," Karl whispered when their eyes met.

Tanny glanced toward the kitchen. "She will scold if I don't keep at my work, Karl."

Karl smiled down into her soft blue eyes. "I hope you won't always have to work for her. But—here." He fished a tiny package from his pocket. "I got this for you today. I hope you like it."

Her questioning look met his, then returned to the packet she held in her hands. After another quick glance at the kitchen door, she opened it. There, amid the folds of paper, lay the most delicate, lacy handkerchief Karl had ever seen. Only for a second had he questioned parting with so much of his daily wage to purchase it.

The expression on Tanny's face made the gift worth every penny! "Oh, thank you, Karl. It's lovely!" Impulsively she reached out and gave his arm a gentle squeeze. "I'll treasure this forever, really I will!"

Karl nearly floated up the stairs. He could still feel her hand on his arm and he longed for another quiet moment to spend with her.

But when Karl opened the door to his room his joy vanished. There sat Enoch, just staring at the wall. In times past evenings had been pleasant social times for the two friends. Now all that had changed, for since their quarrel about Zachary things had gone downhill. In his gentle way Enoch kept trying to convince Karl that there was something suspicious about Zachary. Angry at Enoch's "mother hen" act, Karl often blurted out things that he later regretted. Eventually a stiff silence had settled over the room as they first bristled, then tried to stay out of each other's way. Sometimes Karl even found himself wishing that Enoch had already returned to Modesto.

One evening when Karl felt he could stand the prickly atmosphere no longer, he thankfully accepted a surprise dinner invitation from Zachary, leaving Enoch slumped on his bed. To Karl's surprise, Zachary chose one of the fine restaurants near city center—one with snowy tablecloths and flickering candles in scarlet pots. Karl felt awed over such elegance and uneasy about his country manners. So he watched Zachary's every move, from the way he addressed the waiter to how he spread his napkin in his lap instead of tucking it into his collar. Quick to learn, Karl did his best to follow his host's example.

Never before had he imagined such delicate food as appeared on his plate. Never had he eaten to a background of soft chamber music. Now he knew even more reasons to become wealthy.

When they both had eaten their fill, a uniformed lad carried their plates away and Zachary leaned back and smiled. "I think we'll make a city gent out of you yet, Karl. Getting up in the world demands rubbing shoulders with the wealthy, which you'll have to do when you start working for me. To do that one must acquire a knowledge of fine manners." He took something from his breast pocket.

Karl nodded as he arose.

"Where you going?"

Karl paused. "It's getting late. Shouldn't we head home?"

Zachary chuckled. "We have to wait for the check. Besides, I always like a smoke after my meal, but you know how Mrs. Bidley feels about that. Join me?"

Karl sank back into the chair. "Nah," he said, embarrassed about nearly walking out before they'd paid. Funny, he hadn't realized that Zachary partook of the weed. Not that it bothered him. It was just that Pa had always insisted smoking was a wasteful habit and he hadn't thought of Zachary as wasteful.

"Might as well roll up your dollar bill and puff on it," Pa had often remarked. "Smoking doesn't accomplish anything except making you stink and emptying your pocket."

Zachary opened his gold case and selected a cigarette. He tapped it on the back of his hand, then struck a match. Karl watched the little stick burst into flame. Then the waiter brought the dinner check.

Karl eyed the bill Zachary tossed onto the tray. He would never pay that much for a meal! But Zachary looked as though it were nothing. He was so comfortable and sure of himself, making Karl painfully aware of his farm upbringing.

Suddenly Karl was eager to get out of the place, to be back with his own kind. But Zachary seemed in no hurry to leave. He studied Karl through the smoke that wafted upward from his cigarette. Then he took out the little gold case again.

"Have a go at one of these. You can always put it out if you don't like it."

In his mind's eye Karl imagined Ma's face if she should learn he took even one puff. But he was no child! He was a man—on his own! This was *his* decision.

Perhaps Zachary sensed Karl's dilemma for he grew quite serious. "You know, I don't care if you smoke or not. But tell me, what do you plan to do when you're closing a deal with a rich businessman someday and he offers you a cigarette? Turn it down and offend him? Or take it and choke to death because you don't know how to smoke?"

"W-well—"

Zachary slid the case across the table. "Then why not give it a go?"

Pa's admonitions about the evils of the city nibbled at him. But with Zachary watching, and not wanting to seem immature, Karl finally selected one of the smooth brown cigarettes.

Later Karl bade Zachary a pleasant goodnight and tiptoed to his room, somehow feeling more independent than ever. Inside, the lamp flickered, and its cozy light danced across the lump that Enoch made in his bed. Karl undressed quietly, inwardly proud of how he had handled his first cigarette. He recalled its smoothness between his fingers and Zackary's admiration because he smoked the whole thing without choking once.

Karl blew out the lamp and crawled into bed, not bothering about prayers. After he had settled down, Enoch's quiet voice broke the stillness. "Iffin' I didn't know you b-better, I'd say you'd been smoking."

Suddenly uncomfortable again, Karl pretended to be asleep.

There was a long pause. "Wonder what yer Pa'd say—an' yer Ma."

Karl clenched his fists beneath the bed covers. Why couldn't Enoch just let things be? Karl tried to squelch the guilty feeling that crowded in on him. He was his own man! He could make his own decisions now. He didn't need Enoch for an extra conscience tagging him around, telling him what not to do!

"Shut up," he growled before turning his face to the wall.

The next Sunday Karl went to church with Tanny instead of with Enoch. Her church was larger and its members dressed like the people he'd watched go into restaurants. As they sat with her mother in the pew, Karl became very aware of Tanny with her delicate perfume and her soft breathing. Her tiny hands rested in her lap as she listened to the preacher. He eyed those hands, desperately wanting to take one of them in his, but he knew it would be dreadfully improper and besides, her mother would have a fit.

In spite of the distractions, the pastor's words somehow made their way through Karl's feelings and into his brain. He preached of the importance of keeping a clean slate—of constantly living in such a way that they would be ready to meet Jesus. He painted a word picture of the end of the world—a time when Christ would return to take home only those who had lived a clean and kindly life on earth. It was important, the preacher insisted, to be prepared for that time. He urged his congregation to put away their differences, and to treat each other with loving kindness, as Christ would treat His neighbor if He walked the streets of San Francisco.

In the quietness of the sanctuary Karl remembered his former brotherhood with Enoch, how they had stood up for each other during hard times, and how they'd been able to share their deepest feelings. Increasingly uncomfortable about the wall that had grown between them, he determined to do whatever he must to restore their former relationship. He glanced at Tanny, recalling her puzzled remarks about his estrangement with Enoch. As his conscience prodded he determined to follow the preacher's advice—he would forgive Enoch for all his nagging and his tendency to pass quick judgment on people he didn't understand. Then he would be ready when the terrible things the preacher predicted came to pass.

After church Karl asked Tanny if she and her mother could accompany him for a stroll later in the day.

Tanny smiled tenderly. "I wish we could, but my aunt and her family are arriving this afternoon. It's the only time I'll be able to visit with them for they plan to leave in the morning."

Disappointed, Karl trudged back to the rooming house, and as he walked the urgency of the preacher's words gradually faded. As though waking from a dream that had nearly swallowed him, he discovered that the streets of San Francisco seemed as normal as ever. Suddenly, the preacher's predictions seemed preposterous. Karl couldn't imagine that Jesus' coming was anywhere near, though he allowed it would happen some far-off day.

The way things stood now, he reasoned, Enoch had quit harping on his relationship with Zachary. But if Karl tried to mend the rift, no doubt Enoch would start playing conscience for him again. Karl had left home to get away from people who tried to decide his future and ended out with a nagging roommate instead. It was no bargain.

Karl shook off the uncomfortable thought of Jesus' sudden return, of Jesus' knowing that he still held hard feelings against Enoch. Surely it couldn't happen that quickly. After all, Karl needed time to prove to Pa that he was his own man. Jesus couldn't come before he got his own rig! More than anything, not before he and Tanny had an understanding.

Karl trudged up the rooming house steps. No, this wasn't the time to worry about confessing sins or healing old wounds. There just wasn't time for that. Not when he was stepping into manhood, and his future looked so rosy.

Wednesday, April 18, began like all other working days for Karl. Waking at 3:30, he fumbled around in the darkness for his pants and shirt and dressed quietly so that Enoch could sleep a couple hours longer before Mrs. Bidley wakened him. Then with boots in hand, he tiptoed down the creaky stairs and perched on the front steps to tie his laces.

The pre-dawn chill wrapped around him, thoroughly waking him after his short night of sleep. Though his rest had been much too brief, he eagerly looked forward to the long trek to the docks for it was a good time to sort out his thoughts and to think about Tanny. His heart lurched at the thought of her. She'd be away visiting family for three whole days. And three days was a long time to go without seeing her.

But the friendly fog swirled around him, enfolding him in his own private world as he hurried down the hills, past the gas lamps which made bright spots along the street. It seemed that life would go on this way forever, busy and secure, and with the promise of wonderful things to come.

For once the wagon was ready to go before Karl arrived. "Hurry your deliveries this morning, m'boy," Mr. Tweedy called over the commotion of loading another wagon. "There's a big order for this afternoon and we'll need an early start."

Karl doffed his cap and climbed into the wagon. At a flick

of the reins, old Jacob leaned into the harness and soon the metallic clip-clop of horseshoes echoed a steady tattoo against the ferry building as the team hurried along the waterfront. Karl glanced up at the clock. The black hands showed 4:54. With Mr. Tweedy's words still ringing in his ears, Karl snapped the whip above the horses backs, hoping to gain a few precious seconds.

They swung onto Market Street, slowing as they inched up the steep hill, but at last they reached the crest and picked up speed again. The fog had receded, and early morning light filtered between the tall buildings, casting a bluish sheen onto the storefronts.

Once on the level, Karl sucked in a cool breath and glanced toward the curb. Other draymen were already unloading their wares, and here and there along the street an energetic proprietor swept his front walk.

A young woman with two children at her heels hurried along the walk ahead of him. On her arm she carried a large wicker basket. Somehow she reminded him of Tanny. Automatically he reached into his pocket for his breakfast roll. But there was none, for Tanny was away.

Suddenly a scream sliced through the everyday sounds. Hair on end, Karl glanced over his shoulder to see who was in trouble, but he could spot nothing amiss. Then his wagon lurched as though pushed aside by some great, rough hand, and the horses stumbled as though drugged.

Karl clutched the seat to steady himself. Beside them a store sign was wrenched from its hooks and slammed to the sidewalk. Startled, old Jacob leapt forward, pulling his teammates off balance. As they struggled to regain their footing Karl snubbed up on the reins. And then the roadway ahead rose and buckled.

In vain Karl tried to hold the team back, but they were spooked by the moving road, falling debris, and the screams of people who rushed from second-story apartments in their night clothes.

"Earthquake!" someone shouted. And it was echoed all along the street.

And then the window in Watson's Apparel Shoppe shattered, sending old Jacob into a new frenzy. So fast Karl didn't have time to think, the pavement opened, and right before his eyes gaped wider and wider. Old Jacob saw it too, and swerved sharply, nearly upsetting the wagon in his effort to avoid the jagged hole. But it was too late, for by then the stumbling team had picked up speed and was totally out of control.

Karl watched in helpless horror as the horses nosed into the crevices. Instinctively, he flung himself over the side of the wagon. Time stood still as he hung in mid-air. And then he slammed to the earth. The street writhed beneath him as though it were alive. It complained with a low, raspy grating. Above the commotion Karl heard the horses scream in terror. Then, as suddenly as it had started, the earthquake stopped.

For a moment he lay upon the littered roadway, his breath clutched in a fist of pain. All was silent. Then the cries began again.

Karl forced himself to his feet, ignoring his skinned hands and knees and the searing pain in his side. Frantically he looked to where his wagon had just been. All he could see of his outfit was the tailboard of the wagon and its rear wheels spinning.

"The horses!" he cried, stumbling toward the ragged hole. Stomach lurching, he looked, unwilling to accept the fact that the animals he had come to love would be suffering. Automatically he reached out and stopped the spinning wheel, then holding back a retch, turned from the gruesome scene. There had been no movement in the hole below. No sound. It was too late. There was nothing he could do for the horses.

Then the earth shifted again, and a new shout rang out. "It's falling!"

In terror Karl glanced at the three-story dry goods store just ahead, and watched in awe as its heavy sign wrenched free and slammed to the ground.

Then, as though made from children's building blocks, the front wall collapsed. Instantly, the preacher's predictions came to Karl's mind. Had he been right? Was the world coming to an end—right now? Automatically, Karl darted away from the toppling structure, tripped over a cat, and ground his bleeding hands into the pavement once more.

He lay there for what seemed hours, until the ground quieted and the aftershock ended. Then he struggled to his feet, stiff and sore. Dazed women scurried about in the street, calling to their children. Men tore at the wreckage of buildings that had just collapsed. A confused store proprietor went back to sweeping his littered front walks.

Dust was still rising when a small yellow flame licked between the boards of the collapsed dry goods store. Karl yanked his jacket off and picked his way across the street. A couple other men followed his example, and together they tried to smother the flames. But the fire reached upward, crackling to life, growing too fast for men and their pitifully useless coats.

"The gas lines!" someone yelped, and then, from somewhere up the street came a muffled explosion. The tiny flame expanded fast, fed by the the dangerous leak. A man tore at the boards, sobbing a woman's name.

"This is crazy," Karl yelped as he swallowed his fear and rushed to help the man. But there was no use, for moments later the scorching fire forced them both away from the ruins. In quick succession smaller fires popped up all along the street, crackling and hungry, spreading so fast that Karl knew everyone must soon leave the area.

Smoke clawed at his lungs as he turned toward the waterfront. Coughing, and eyes smarting, he squinted toward the Ferry Tower. Between bellows of black smoke that belched from the buildings below, Karl spotted the Ferry Tower. The clock hands pointed at 5:16, though he knew it was later. Perhaps the hands stopped when the quake hit.

Suddenly a terrible thought hit him—Mrs. Bidley didn't waken Enoch until 5:30. During the quake his roommate would still have been in bed.

With thoughts of the wooden boardinghouse that perched on the hillside, Karl began to run through the rubble-filled streets. His anger toward Enoch vanished and worry took its place. Now the confusion around him meant nothing—the frightened people's cries for help fell on deaf ears, for he had only one thought. He must go at once to find Enoch, his dearest friend.

But as he stumbled along Karl's hope dwindled, for on every side buildings had tumbled. Buildings that had not collapsed from the earthquake's violence now blazed because of gas escaping from broken lines. Cries of terror rang out above the sounds of raging fires.

Karl pelted down the hill, barely glancing at Tanny's place when he passed. How glad he felt that she and her family had gone on their short holiday. To think he had begrudged them the time away.

At last Karl turned the corner and stared at what had been his home for the past couple of months. The front part of the building had fallen away, leaving the back wall of his room exposed. He spied his red and black checkered shirt, still hanging on its peg, as though nothing at all had happened. Boards and plaster, like spilled matchsticks, lay in a tortured pile that stretched across the street. A twisted metal bedstead poked from the debris, and one of Mrs. Bidley's colorful bed quilts lay, ripped and dirty, in a tangled heap of boards.

The horrible truth pressed down upon Karl, so heavy he could hardly keep from crying out. Zachary would have been up, but most of the men he ate with every night, the ones who slept under the same roof, would not yet have left for work when the quake hit. He scanned the rubble. Were they under that awful heap of building materials?

Gulping back his tears, Karl scanned the faces around him, but of course Enoch was not there. At that moment he noticed a sooty-faced woman standing alone, wooden spoon in hand. It was a second before he recognized her, but when he did he scrambled to her side.

"Mrs. Bidley, where's Enoch?"

Her dazed eyes flicked across his face as though he were a stranger. Then she held up her spoon. "And it was a lovely breakfast I was making, too."

Then the ground shifted again. Another board swung loose, and as it dropped, Karl grabbed Mrs. Bidley's fleshy arm and pulled her away.

"No" she screamed, swatting him with her spoon as she wrenched free.

Karl grabbed her again and forced her across the street in spite of her blows.

"Enoch!" he screamed. "Have you seen Enoch?"

She yanked away once more and wandered back toward the boarding house.

And then Karl noticed a slender white thread of smoke rising from the debris. Suddenly it burst into flames. The gas had found a spark and would now do its work. Dark sadness such as he had never known before gripped him. There was nothing he nor anyone else could do to change things. Even prayer wouldn't help now. Enoch was beneath the pile of burning rubble. Carl sucked in his breath as the truth hit him. *Enoch's end-of-the-world had come!*

Soon the heat from the hungry flames drove him back, so Karl turned toward the waterfront, walking automatically, hardly seeing the terrified people or the bricks and mortar or new fires that licked hungrily at every side. He had never experienced panic before—but now it surrounded him, thick enough to touch. He must leave—must get away from the orange death, the screaming voices, the sight of broken bodies lying in the street.

Why had he ever come to the city? He wanted nothing more to do with it! He *longed* to go home—home to the farm where the air was clean, where the corn stood in orderly rows, and where he'd be surrounded by nothing more dangerous than slobbering cows.

His mind made up, he stumbled toward the ferry landing. Then abruptly, Enoch's face took form in his mind, the shy but gentle face of the boy who had been his best friend. What had he always said?

"*Live for others.*" That's what Enoch always did—had been doing for him too, though Karl had refused to admit it. Now it was too late to apologize for the way he'd treated his friend.

Karl choked back a sob. Why, if Enoch were alive he wouldn't go running off. He'd think it cowardly to slink away when others needed his help so much. There was no way he could make things up to Enoch, but he *could* be Enoch's hands—do what Enoch would have done if he were still alive.

He glanced around. The whole city lay in confusion. He turned first one way, then another, trying to find his way through the blocked streets. Where should he begin to help? What could he do to change things?

"God, please show me," he sobbed.

It seemed as though his mind cleared then, and all at once he knew what he must do first. He must go to the dock and find his boss—tell him about the team. Mr. Tweedy would know what to do.

His mind made up, he hurried down the long hill and past the Ferry Building, now cracked but still standing. Beyond it lay the wall of an old warehouse, draped like a piece of cloth over a docked ship. As he sped toward Mr. Tweedy's place, he noticed that the damage grew less and less—this part of the city seemed almost normal.

After what seemed hours he spotted Mr. Tweedy with a group of men, and he rushed toward him and blurted out the fate of the team.

Mr. Tweedy's shoulders sagged. "Jacob's been with me a long time—but never mind that, m'boy." He shook his head, as though to clear a fog. Then he studied Karl. "What's important is that you didn't go down with 'em. Say, you've got a nasty cut on your face. You hurt anywhere else?"

"No," Karl fibbed, ignoring the ache in his shoulder and the throbbing in his side. There was no time to worry about little hurts when there was so much destruction around them.

A determined look crossed Mr. Tweedy's face. "Very well. Officer O'Grady just left. He's asked us to help organize the men here and have 'em drive along the fringes of the damaged areas. Need to pick up the injured. He said they're setting up an emergency hospital at the Mechanics' Pavillion. Everything's all right over there." He glanced at the smoky sky and shook his head.

"All but one of my wagons were out, and Reb has already gone with it. But Fish Willy says we can use the two he's got. Will you help us move people to the Pavillion, m'boy?"

Karl gulped. He didn't want to hear the cries of frightened people or see any more mangled bodies, But there wasn't time to coddle his own desires. He'd asked God what he should do, and for strength to do it. Couldn't he trust Him to provide it?

12

Within a few minutes Karl perched in one of Fish Willy's smelly wagons, urging the skittish team through restless crowds to the rim of the disaster areas. Though only minor damage had occurred on the street where he drove, the place seethed with folk who had escaped from the hardest-hit section of the city. On the side streets, men, scurrying like the sand crabs he'd seen on the beach, climbed over rubble in search of missing loved ones.

Karl watched in horror as men tied cloths over their noses and forced themselves down smoky lanes, ripping at piles of debris, crying out for help when they found a trapped person still alive. Gentle hands placed the injured on the sidewalks of the bordering streets. Wives sobbed into their dusty handkerchiefs while husbands stroked wispy hair from pale brows. A woman lay near the curb, her bodice crimson. Two towheaded youngsters sobbed over her, calling her name, pressing her pale, quiet hands to their faces, but she did not move.

Seeing the injured children was hardest for Karl. The lucky ones—those who had the energy—cried loudly. Others lay limp and gray in their mother's arms, many still dressed in their flannel nightgowns. But here and there a child sat alone, watching the activity in stunned silence. Karl swallowed hard.

How would they find family survivors? What would become of them?

Wave after wave of acrid smoke engulfed Karl as he drove up the hill to his assigned area. Tears gushed from his smarting eyes and he hunched forward to stifle his cough, for pain shot through his chest like lightning when he did.

He clamped his lower lip between his teeth and urged the horses onward through the sea of frightened humanity. The team had barely picked up speed when a little white dog raced across the street, nose to the ground. He sniffed frantically at the people he passed, obviously searching for someone.

Karl swallowed hard. "Good luck, little dog," he whispered.

There had been no real breakfast that morning, but now the tragedy surrounding him fought with his stomach, and the carrot he'd munched while riding in the wagon, threatened to come up. He clutched the reins, swallowed hard, and willed himself onward. But control was hard to maintain. Suddenly he had an overwhelming urge to jump out of the wagon and run for all he was worth—run until his lungs were filled with clean air again, run to a place where children laughed in the morning sunshine and the crazy world ended all its madness. *Grab hold!* he scolded himself. He couldn't give in to feelings now. Now was the time for action!

Karl swiped the tears from his cheeks. Then quickly and carefully he filled Fish Willy's wagon with burn victims and injured children and headed back down the long hill and toward the pavilion.

At the pavilion things were better. There had been little damage to the buildings in that section of the city and the fires were far away. Many volunteers came to help the doctors and nurses who somehow organized working units. Men met each wagon, hurrying the most severely injured to one part of the grounds, the minor casualties to another. To his surprise Karl spotted Navy doctors and nurses in their uniforms. How quickly they had arrived from Mare Island which poked from the water between San Francisco and Oakland!

Catholic Sisters and Salvation Army lasses swarmed the place as well, stooping over the injured, comforting crying children, and aiding in any way they could.

Time after time Karl made the long journey up the hill to collect the injured, then turned back toward the pavilion. As he picked up his passengers, he searched each face, hoping by some miracle to stumble upon Enoch. Heavy-hearted and silent, he went about his work of mercy, thinking of his missing friend. *God, why couldn't You have saved Enoch? I promise, I'd never feel cross with him again, even if he stuck his nose in where it didn't belong! I'd leave cigarettes alone and go to church each week. . . . * Karl's thoughts and prayers tumbled through his mind. But even as he looked, hoped, and vowed, he knew it was useless. Enoch could not have lived through the collapse of the flimsy building, nor the fire which consumed it.

Each time Karl completed a trip the fire had eaten closer to the pavilion, greedily devouring the wooden buildings in its pathway. The acrid smoke burned his eyes, clawed at his throat. But still he would not give up. As the day ground on, sooty flakes sifted down from the great black cloud which hovered over the city, making it look like pictures Karl had seen of the end of the world. He shuddered as he eyed the destruction. Dozens of buildings had burned to the ground, and though the fire fighters did their best to stop the advancing flames, even to the point of dynamiting some buildings to create a firebreak, the hungry flames licked onward until they finally nibbled at the edges of the pavilion.

A ghostly pallor hid the afternoon sun. Would the walks never be emptied of injured to load into the fishy wagon? Where did the men who still scrambled over the rubble keep finding victims? Thirst had long since swelled his tongue and the tears that flowed and helped clean the smoke from his eyes had virtually stopped. But there was no time to search for water. No time to stop and rest his own aching body. Only time to press onward—to make one more round trip before the horses finally refused to budge.

Early that afternoon as Karl pulled into the pavilion, a policeman ran to meet him. "Turn back! We're evacuating!" he shouted, waving his arms. "Fire's too close! We're moving everyone to Golden Gate Park!"

Karl gulped. The park was miles away, and he was hauling some dreadfully injured people. Was there time to get them so far?

A doctor carrying a child hurried toward Karl's wagon and peered inside. "There's more room here!" he bellowed over his shoulder. His face was caked with blood and streaked with ashes, but there was a tender look on his face as he settled the little one on the wagon floor. Several others were loaded in, too. Then the policeman hollered, "Hurry now, and mind you don't get cut off by the fire!"

The street leading from the pavilion swarmed with frantic people trying to escape the hungry flames. Their arms were loaded with an odd assortment of goods they had salvaged from their homes. So many people jammed the street that they blocked the route the wagons must travel. Clouds of sparks and hot ashes blew overhead. Hot cinders rained down upon the frightened people and horses. Then a fire broke out directly ahead! Instantly the sea of people tried to turn back, rushing toward Karl and his passengers.

"We've got to get off this street!" Karl shouted as he struggled to control the horses. Through the sea of people he spotted a road that led to the waterfront. He cracked the whip, urging the team into the oncoming crowd. Then the wind changed, and gusts of black smoke blew down between the houses and across the street, making the horses even more skittish.

Karl swiped at his eyes. All it would take to spook the uneasy horses was a falling timber or an explosion. Then they would bolt in fear, trampling anyone in their pathway, and putting the injured passengers at even more risk.

As the roar of the nearby fire increased fear tingled down Karl's spine. His eyes felt as though someone had buffed them with sandpaper. Hunger tore at his middle, and the urge to save himself was strong. Yet he knew he couldn't abandon his passengers.

Just then something in the next block exploded! Flames shot high into the sky, Fish Willy's team reared, then plunged as screams filled the air. Karl tugged on the reins with all his might in an effort to control the horses. Then someone from behind poked him. "Blinders," the man croaked, pushing a blood-crusted jacket onto the seat. Shawls and a baby blanket quickly followed.

Karl struggled to hold the team in check as he eyed the oncoming crowd. He had to get help!

"Hey, Mac," he hollered to a brawny teenager struggling toward them.

The boy didn't hear.

"You, there! Please help!"

Their glances met. "I've got injured folks—horses spooking—need to cover their eyes."

The boy nodded, and as Karl tugged on the reins, the young man grabbed the jacket and somehow tied it around the head of the closest horse so he couldn't see the surrounding confusion.

Then the boy reached for the blanket. "You're going the wrong way! Pavilion's behind you!"

"They turned us away! Moving everyone to Golden Gate Park."

When the blanket covered the second horse's eyes, Karl's

helper backed away. But then the horses wouldn't budge.

Karl couldn't let the boy leave, for it would take two to do what was necessary. "Please come hold the reins while I try to lead the horses to that side street," he suggested.

Without hesitation the boy climbed up and grabbed the leather straps. Karl eased down, stroking the nearest horse as he worked his way to its head. Its sweaty flesh quivered beneath his hand. "Easy, boy," Karl crooned. He grasped the bridle and began to inch forward. At first the horses didn't want to cooperate, but Karl kept talking and soon the frightened beasts calmed enough to be led through the crowd.

After what seemed hours, they turned onto the side street and Karl breathed a sigh of relief.

"You'll be all right now," said the boy as he looked back at the busy street they'd just left. "I hafta go look for someone."

Karl uncovered the horses eyes and climbed back into the wagon. Then the boy vaulted over the side and disappeared into the crowd.

Funny. In church with Enoch, Karl had heard about angels who came to help people. They always disappeared quickly and left people wondering. But the preacher had also said that God used ordinary people to do His work. Maybe God had sent that boy!

Very little traffic moved toward the park. Many steep hills lay between it and where Karl's team plodded. But there his passengers would be safe, for there were no buildings to burn or tumble down upon them. But night was not far away. With no shelter at the park how would the injured make the night? Most of them were still in lightweight sleepwear and the cold, clammy fog would roll in as soon as the sun dropped behind the bay.

Karl heaved a sigh and urged the horses on. After awhile they passed the hill where he had lived. Tears stung his eyes as he scanned the skyline. So many fires still raged, so much black smoke belched upward. Maybe it would keep on burning until there was nothing left at all!

Suddenly an awful thought struck him. The preacher had been right. For hundreds of people the end of the world had come that very day. Just this morning they had been alive, and now—a sob clawed at his throat. The world had ended for Enoch, too.

Then, in his mind's eye the awful black hole that had claimed his team that morning opened up again, wide enough to swallow the rig and himself too. He shook his head, forcing the horrible memory away. He wasn't the one that was good and kind. He was nothing but selfish. Why had he been spared and Enoch lost?

Grimly, he forced back the sobs that tried to break free. He had a task at hand. There was no time to think about what had happened.

Through the long afternoon and into the night he labored on, picking up and moving moaning wagonloads of people. Each time he neared the park, relief that they had escaped the raging fires once more flooded over him. The fresh winds which blew in from the sea, though chilly, were a Godsend, for they kept the choking smoke away.

There was no way to tell the time, for in his leap from the wagon he had smashed his pocket watch. He knew only that the sky's brightness was caused by fires rather than the sun. Close to exhaustion, Karl forced himself and the team to keep going. Once a woman pressed a boiled potato into his hand, but he couldn't eat it. No matter how busy his hands, his mind kept turning back to poor Enoch trapped beneath the rubble, no doubt burned to ashes by now.

His stomach churned each time he thought about how alone and frightened his friend must have felt. Had he lived for a time after the earthquake, before the fires came? Had he been terrified, buried under the rubble, before the fire? Or had he, mercifully, been knocked unconscious when the boarding house fell? How he dreaded preparing the telegram he knew he must send Enoch's mother!

It must have been past midnight when he turned away from the park and headed back toward town. Now only a few wagons rolled in, bringing their sad cargo. The pavilion had long since been emptied of its injured and was nothing more than a pile of ashes. Slumped in his seat, his eyes so swollen he could hardly see, Karl paid little attention to his surroundings.

Then someone shouted his name and hope flared up again. Karl peered into the darkness as a wagon creaked up beside him. The driver's face was black with soot, his eyes ringed with white where smarting tears had washed the dirt away.

"I see you've kept busy, too!" called Zachary, his voice raspy. "Where will you sleep tonight?"

Karl focused on the idea. He'd been so busy he hadn't thought of where he would sleep, or even if he would. Suddenly he felt very thankful that he was looking into the face of someone he knew and cared about, someone who could help him put his thoughts to rights.

"Dunno. Don't know when we can stop."

Zachary coughed. "There's not much else we can do—too dark. These are the last of the folks that were along the street." Then Zachary grinned, and his teeth made a white slice in the darkness.

"I see you're driving Fish Willy's worthy chariot—in fact, I could have told you that with my eyes shut." He gave a short, harsh laugh. "How about meeting at his place after I've dropped these folk off? You're going to return the team, aren't you?"

Karl nodded.

Zachary thumped the side of his wagon. "At least I've still got my rig. We can sleep in here 'til we find something better."

"It's a deal!" called Karl as he flicked the reins and the

horses reluctantly moved forward again. As he jostled down the dark street, his mind whirled. He should be feeling happy to have a place to stay. Why was it that just now he had to remember how much Enoch had distrusted Zachary, and to feel that his friend—now gone—would be displeased with the arrangements if he knew about them?

Karl shuddered as the wagon, still smelling of fish and now of smoke and death, rattled into the darkness.

13

As Karl drove the wagon onto the pier, Fish Willy arose from the crate where he'd been resting. Light from several rag torches flickered across his haggard face, making him look ancient and worn, but he moved toward Karl and the team quickly. Clucking soft words to the exhausted beasts, he began the task of unharnessing them so they could bed down in their makeshift home for what remained of the night.

Though Karl felt too tired to move he forced his weary muscles into action. Aching, he climbed from the wagon and scooped out oats for each horse, but when he led them to their meal, their heads drooped in weariness, and they gave only a disinterested sniff to the food they usually loved.

"They's right tuckered," clucked Fish Willy. He squinted at Karl. "You, too."

"Everyone is," Karl mumbled.

The old man sighed. "What you gonna do tomorry, boy?"

"Guess I'll see if I can find out anything about the roomers in my boarding house—see if any made it. I saw my landlady —she was pretty mixed up and wouldn't leave the area. That was before the fire got real bad."

Fish Willy pulled a rag from his pocket and started rubbing down the closest horse. "They's settin' up a registry in that old church, y'know. Lookin' for anyone special?"

The knot in Karl's stomach cinched up. "My—my best friend. We came here together."

Fish Willy nodded sympathetically. "Well, you jist ask there'n I wager you'll find 'im."

Just then Zachary's team rumbled onto the wooden dock. "Hey, Fish!" he called, "mind if I tie up here for the night?"

Fish Willy peered at the newcomer, then nodded. "Help yerself to feed'n water. Stuff's over there."

A while later Karl settled down in the dirty wagon beside Zachary. The thick blankets that usually protected trunks were stiff with bloodstains and reeked of smoke and sweat, but Karl was too exhausted to let that matter. Blankets of any kind would provide protection from the misty morning chill that had settled over the city. With a weary sigh, he fell into a dreamless sleep.

The sun had already risen before Karl awoke the next morning. At first, in that hazy place between sleep and wakefulness, he thought Enoch was sitting on his chest. Annoyed at his roommate's practical joke, he pushed against the weight. Pain shot through his shoulder and side. But there was something else. The sounds were not boardinghouse sounds but those of lapping water and muffled voices and heavy footsteps against planking.

An awful stench filled his nostrils. Confused, he forced his eyes to open and focused on the wagon sideboards. Only then did he remember the day that had just passed. With a catch in his throat, he realized that his chest-weight was not caused by Enoch but by his leap from the wagon, and from breathing smoke and coughing the day before.

Karl pushed the crusty blanket away and groaned as he tried to sit up. Every movement was agony. His hands felt stiff as starched shirt collars and his smoke-raw eyes gushed with tears. But now fresh breezes blew in from the bay which lapped at the pier, and the bit of smoke that still wafted from the ruins was whisked away from the waterfront. Carefully, Karl sucked in a deep breath. The clean air tasted good.

Zachary poked his head over the wagon side. "Someone here to see you," he said as cheerily as if nothing unusual had happened.

Wild joy leapt within Karl! It would be Enoch, well and alive—saved by God after all! In spite of his pain, he forced himself up and peered over the wagon side, eager to see Enoch's crooked grin for himself. But again disappointment crushed down upon him, for it was Mr. Tweedy's watery blue eyes that met his.

The old man reached out and tousled Karl's hair. "Glad to see you made it, m'boy. I was plumb worried that you got caught up in them fires that took th' pavilion down!"

Karl grinned in spite of his disappointment. Funny how you could be glad and sad all at the same time. Glad to see Mr. Tweedy, who suddenly seemed very dear to him, and dying inside because of the truth about Enoch.

Mr. Tweedy came right to the point. "In spite of this crazy place tumblin' round our ears, people still gotta eat. I been checkin' and most of our suppliers can still get their produce to us, but all my drivers' ceptin' you have left town. You willin' to stick by 'n lend a hand so's we can feed this city? We still have two wagons."

The word "we" stuck in Karl's mind as he struggled out of the wagon. Hadn't Enoch predicted that Mr. Tweedy would take him into the business—just like a son? Though his inclination was to turn his back on the problems around him and head straight for home, his duty, clear and simple, was to help out where he could. And what could be more important than helping Mr. Tweedy provide food for hungry people?

Karl wiped his smarting eyes. "I'd be—"

"Wait!" Zachary demanded, stepping between them. "I've got something to say to Karl before he answers you."

Mr. Tweedy's watery eyes settled on Zachary. "Say on."

Zachary steered Karl toward the end of the pier, out of earshot. "I had a bit of good luck yesterday—made a good deal on another wagon."

He shook his head. "Man lost his whole family so he sold it to me for the price of a train ticket home. Thought maybe you could start working for me now, Karl, like we talked about before. No better time to start making your fortune than the present—right when people need their things moved."

He glanced toward Mr. Tweedy, then lowered his voice. "There's enough demand that we could keep two wagons going day and night if we had that kind of energy. Fact is, I'll pay you by the load at the end of each day. You'll make twice as much as Tweedy'll ever offer you."

Karl thought about Grandpap's old money sock which he'd kept beneath his mattress. With it gone he hadn't a nickel to his name and he surely needed money now. He glanced at Mr. Tweedy, his rumpled clothing stained, his hair a wild mess. It was hard to see him suffering. Fish Willy had told him the night before that Mr. Tweedy had lost most everything—his home, two teams and wagons. It seemed a shame to desert him now, but what else could he do?

Karl had suffered too. He'd lost Enoch, his clothes, his money sock. He needed quick cash. He glanced down at his dirty, torn shirt. He couldn't go back to Modesto like this. It was time to get practical. He shoved his sentimental feelings aside and nodded to Zachary. "I'll tell Tweedy I've already accepted another position."

Mr. Tweedy's gentle but disappointed eyes made Karl feel terrible, but the old man accepted Karl's decision kindly, like the Christian gentleman Karl knew him to be. "I wish y' luck, m'boy. Yer a good worker and it's no wonder Polson's a'fightin' to get you." His sad smile held warmth as he gave Karl's shoulders a quick squeeze. "God go with you."

Karl gulped and turned back to Zachary, who looked smugly satisfied.

Twice on the day following the earthquake Karl stopped at the registry. Lines of people made an ever-moving fringe along the street as they inched toward the tables that had been set up in the church foyer. There they scanned names of others who had signed the books, and then wrote their own. Both times Karl reached the table his hopes soared. Surely God couldn't have let Enoch die. But as he watched the clerk's finger trace the columns of names and saw him shake his head, disappointment came smashing down again. Each hour his dread deepened. It was bad enough to lose his best friend, but now he faced the task of wiring both his and Enoch's parents. One mother would be relieved, the other heartbroken. But he had to do it. With shaking hands, he composed the awful message on a scrap of paper someone handed him and gave it to the man who would send it.

Karl had gone with Zachary to pick up the new wagon. Together they checked out the team, making sure it was properly hitched. Then Zachary pulled a slip of paper from his shirt pocket.

"Go to Sutter Street. Family in the little house at the base of the hill wants to move out near the park. One trip should do it—they don't have much." He turned to leave, then stopped short. "By the way, I've already collected their fee, so you don't need to worry about it. When you've moved them, go to that second address. I've collected there, too. After that, meet me at The Registry."

When Karl reached the tiny cottage, a face appeared in the window, then vanished. A moment later a skinny man, his face pinched with worry, hurried out.

"You the mover?"

Karl eased down. "Yes, sir."

The man held out a roughened hand and smiled. "Name's

Watts. Probably foolish to move, but I just don't trust these hills after what happened yesterday.'' He turned back to the house. ''Anyway, give me a hand and we'll be finished in no time.''

Together they loaded beds, a table and chairs, a rickety old chest of drawers, and a few other simple household goods into the wagon. Then Mrs. Watts and two little girls climbed in.

Karl noticed that the oldest child's front teeth were missing. She looked about 6—Amanda's age. Remembering his little sister made a lump in his throat. How glad he was that his family didn't live in the city. At least *they* were safe on the farm.

As he drove, Karl was stricken by the devastation everywhere. True, the buildings had sustained terrible damage, but it was the homeless that touched his heart. Huddled together along the streets, families sat dry-eyed and sober. Some had a blanket or two. Others had nothing. Salvation Army soup kettles bubbled on several corners and stoop-shouldered people lined up before them. The line moved slowly, the silent survivors gravely accepting the nourishing liquid in any kind of container they could find.

As they approached one such corner the savory aroma filled the air and Karl could stand his hunger no longer. With an apology for the delay, he pulled to a stop beside one of the kettles and gulped some soup. It was the only food he had eaten since the carrot the previous morning.

''We're so fortunate,'' Mr. Watts said later as they unloaded. ''We're all alive and have our things. It cost a fortune to move, but it doesn't matter. A man's got to do the best thing he can for his family. We couldn't ask the good Lord for anything more than our safety.''

Karl nodded. He thought of the pitiful group of children he'd seen near the registry. They searched the faces of all who passed by, hope of finding their loved ones dwindling each minute. The lump in his own throat swelled as he thought of Enoch. Why couldn't he have been as lucky as the Watts family?

That afternoon, in spite of the damage to the city presses, a newspaper came out. While newsboys held the papers high and shouted the headlines, grim earthquake details jumped off the page. That evening Zachary brought one of the papers back to Fish Willy's. Men gathered around while Zachary perched in his wagon and read the grim statistics aloud.

"Says here that approximately 50,000 people were left homeless and there are hundreds dead. No one's to light fires near the earthquake area. I guess there's still a threat of broken gas lines." Zachary turned the page. "Listen to this. 'Two Score Men Escape From Asylum—Still Missing.' " Karl shuddered. No one knew what lunatics might do under these frightening circumstances.

As Zachary read on, Karl was filled with a lonely ache. Enoch often said that things worked out right for people who loved God, but how was any good going to come from all the death around them? Too tired to think anymore, he settled back in Zachary's wagon and pulled up a blanket. He had moved five families that day, lifting heavy furniture in spite of his sore ribs. Now with darkness coming on, he was more than ready to quit.

Then Zachary nudged him. "Here you go," he said, peeling a couple bills from the wad he held.

Karl gulped. It was more money than Mr. Tweedy gave him in a week. He pushed it away. "You'd better count again."

Zachary chuckled. "That's no mistake. I told you I paid well. There's a gold mine out there if we're willing to work when the opportunity's right."

Pleased, Karl tucked the money into his pocket. If he had time tomorrow he'd try to find a shirt in one of the stores that had not been demolished. It would be good to get out of his torn, filthy clothes.

Then Zachary handed Karl a slip of paper. "That's tomorrow's list. Folks in the countryside have opened their

111

homes and barns to the city people. Our job is to get them there."

Karl wondered if the list included any folk as poor as the Watts' family. "How much shall I charge?" he asked, knowing firsthand about empty pockets.

Zachary's mouth tightened. "I told you not to worry about collecting," he snapped. "That's my job. You just get them moved." Then Zachary held up his hands. "Sorry for biting your head off—it's getting to me, I guess."

Karl shrugged. He understood.

Strange how so many people were paying in advance to be moved, Karl mused as he settled down again. Exhausted, he downed the bread and cheese that Zachary had given him, then fell asleep.

It was only a few minutes later that he awoke with a jolt, calling Enoch's name. In his dream he had seen the boarding house walls collapse upon Enoch, then heard him cry for help. Cold sweat, like an army of red ants, prickled up Karl's spine. His heart pounded and his legs trembled. He forced his sore eyes to stay open, knowing if he went back to sleep he might have the nightmare again. He didn't think he could bear it. But his will to stay awake soon weakened and a moment later he flopped back onto the wagon floor, breathed a shuddery sigh, and slept again.

14

During the next two days Karl moved families to the country from sunrise until after dark. Both nights Zachary peeled some bills from his fat roll and handed them to Karl. The third afternoon while moving another family across town, Karl spied Zachary standing on a corner, talking with two men. Glad for that bit of luck, he pulled to the curb to ask the moving price for a widow who had hailed him earlier in the day.

At his call, Zachary darted across the street. "What are you doing here?" he demanded.

While Karl explained the widow's needs, Zachary's scowl deepened. Finally he interrupted with a growl. "Hop down. I want a private word with you."

Puzzled, Karl followed his boss across the street. Then Zachary turned an icy stare on Karl.

"Who are the people in the wagon?"

Karl went cold. "I was heading across town empty and the man hailed me. They were going to my next pick-up area and wanted a lift, so I loaded them in." He pulled a five-dollar piece from his pocket and offered it to Zachary.

Zachary scowled at the coin. "I said *I'd* handle lining up jobs and collecting. How can we make any money charging puny fees like this?"

Karl was astonished! Five dollars was half a week's wages

for many men! Surely that was enough for driving them and their few things across town!

Zachary thrust the coin into his pocket. "Go ahead and deliver his stuff, but don't arrange anything more, you hear? I can see you have a lot to learn if you ever want to go into business for yourself."

Stunned, Karl returned to the wagon. Why should Zachary get so upset because he'd tried to run full both ways across the city—and to earn a bit more? Didn't every penny count, the way Pa had always taught him?

That evening when Karl pulled onto the pier, Zachary was already there, acting as though nothing had happened. As Karl brushed down the horses and cleaned the wagon he watched Zachary from the corner of his eye. Strange how cheerful his boss seemed when so many others were hurting. He noticed Zachary's air of superiority around the other men who also slept in their wagons on the dock, and Karl grew increasingly uneasy.

His troublesome thoughts were erased, however, as he felt the lump of bills in his pocket. If business stayed as good as it had been, it wouldn't be long before he could purchase his own rig. Then he'd haul who he wanted, when he wanted, for whatever price he thought fair. Besides, when he had his own rig he could think more permanently about Tanny, too.

That third evening after the quake Karl decided to see if Tanny had returned. As he threaded his way between the piles of debris that still littered the streets, his eagerness to see her was shadowed by dread because of the news he must share. He knew how much Tanny admired Enoch—and he'd have to tell her. Why must pleasant times always be tinged with sadness? Why couldn't life always have happy endings?

His heart leaped to his throat when he finally turned onto Tanny's street. Golden light spilled from her window! He took the steps three at a time.

At his knock the door burst open as though she had been

114

expecting him. With a happy cry she flew into his arms, warm and alive. "I thought you'd been killed when the boarding house went down," she sobbed into his shoulder. "I've checked the registry again and again but your name wasn't there. Where have you *been?*"

Karl went numb. He took her by the arms and held her back just enough so he could see her dear face. Remorse over worrying her stabbed through him. "Why, I—I never thought about anyone looking for *me* at the registry," he stammered. "I knew *you* were safe because you were out of town. And there's Mrs. Bidley and Mr. Tweedy and Zachary. He couldn't believe his own stupidity. "I've been there several times myself checking for Enoch but never thought to register my name."

"Never mind," Tanny breathed, snuggling against his shoulder. She trembled in his arms. "You're all right and that's all that matters."

They sat on the porch for a long while, watching the night deepen over the city. Here and there in the dusky patchwork, golden squares of light shown from windows of a few undamaged homes. After Karl told her about Enoch he reached for Tanny's hand. It was soft and warm and real in his.

"Tanny, there's something I want to say," he began, suddenly bold enough to share his dreams with her. "You know I hope to own my own rig someday. I'm sure I can make a go of it on my own."

She nodded.

"But it will be a while yet. I lost everything when the boarding house went down, you know."

Her fingers stiffened ever so slightly as she quietly met his gaze. Then she looked down at their hands, and her hair curtained her face.

"I just want you to know that—that I admire you very much. I'd like us to—" He quit, suddenly shy.

It seemed that Tanny knew what Karl wanted to say. She

rested her head on his shoulder and let out a deep, satisfied sigh. "I feel the same way about you, Karl," she murmured. Then she grew somber. "But there's something I have to tell you, though I wish I didn't."

In spite of the sadness he'd just heard in her voice, a joyous warmth filled Karl as he slipped his arm around her waist. It was plain that she cared.

"What is it?" he asked.

"Mother decided we're moving to Aunt Ethel's house."

Karl's stomach lurched. "Clear down to San Jose, where you just *were?*"

Tanny sniffled. "Yes."

He drew her closer, as though he could prevent her leaving. "When?"

Then she was crying, deep tearing sobs. "Tomorrow. It's tomorrow we're moving, I tried to change her mind, but—"

Suddenly the tragedy of the past few days gripped him as never before. Truth was, he'd lost everything! Not only the money he'd so carefully saved and his good friend Enoch, but even Tanny.

"But that's so far away! You could stay—could work!"

Tanny shook her head. "Mother won't let me, Karl. I already asked."

His mind raced ahead, a hundred miles an hour. Maybe they could get married now—find a little place somewhere in the city. He'd work hard, so very hard to take care of her. But no. It wouldn't work—wasn't practical. He had nothing to offer —not yet.

At last she pulled back and faced him, so small—so delicate—so vulnerable. "Will I ever see you again?" she asked, fighting to control her tears.

And then an unspeakable gladness surged through him, and this time he wrapped both arms around her. Tanny really cared.

In spite of the problems that lay ahead, their paths would cross again. He'd see to that!

"Don't worry, little one. I have to help clean up this city, but then, if only you'll say you want me to, I'll come and find you."

Some time later, with a kiss of promise, they said goodbye. At the corner Karl turned back and gazed at his loved one for a long moment, memorizing the tiny form framed in the rectangle of light that glowed in the open door. Then he turned and headed back toward the dock, his happiness all mixed up with the dread of more days of heartbreaking labor and loneliness because of his separation from both Enoch and Tanny.

15

It was slow going as Karl picked his way through the dark rubble-strewn streets. With each step he relived the last moments he'd spent with Tanny, and tucked every word away in his heart. He would never forget the worry in her voice when she said she'd inquired after him. How foolish he had been to cause her such distress because he hadn't thought to register. Pa always said that there was no better time than the present to right an error. He'd stop on the way to the dock to print his name in the register for whatever it was worth.

Half an hour later when he'd added his name to the list in the busy old church, Karl noticed a handful of men clustered around the corner gas lamp. Its golden glow spilled across them. After all the gloom, the light was a welcome sight, and Karl naturally gravitated toward it.

"That's a thievin' price to charge for movin' a few sticks of furniture!" growled a burly fellow as Karl approached. "Them opportunists should be hung!"

"Who moved you, Max?"

Max spat toward the gutter. "Polson's his name—y'know, the dandy who drives that fancy red wagon. All gussied up and smilin' pretty, he is. Nice as pie, too—'til his hand reaches out to grab yer money." Karl's heart lurched as he slipped into a shadowy doorway. He held his breath, afraid to miss the rest of the conversation.

"Polson moved me an' my woman too," chimed in another. Just about cleaned us out. It's gonna be scanty fare fer awhile, I can tell ya that."

"Rumor has it that if them devils is caught in the act, their wagons'll be seized and used by the city to move them that needs it. Newspaper said so. Thirty dollars a load is plain robbery!"

As Karl pressed against the rough wall the cold brick bit into his palms. Thirty dollars! How could anyone take so much from poor families? A months' wages for a short move was outrageous. Karl's heart pounded. What right had Zachary to take advantage of folks who already had too many problems? And to think that he—Karl Johnson—was helping that greedy Zachary fleece them!

Karl clenched his fists as all the little clues he'd ignored earlier arose to taunt him. He should have been suspicious about earning such easy money and about Zachary's caginess regarding the prices he charged. Why, if he'd had any sense at all, he'd have *known*.

Karl peered at the men who continued to exchange their heated opinions. Had he moved any of them for Zachary? What if he were recognized? How could he explain that he hadn't realized what was going on?

Noiselessly, he slipped out of the doorway and headed in the opposite direction. Enoch had been right. And to think he'd wanted to be just like Zachary. How blind could a fellow be? The old familiar anger prickled at his spine. He'd tell Zachary a thing or two. And then he'd go back to Mr. Tweedy and get his old job back.

All the way to Fish Willy's Karl fumed and rehearsed his speech to Zachary. Nearing the bay, he watched the fog pull itself over the city as though it were a blanket covering scars left by the earthquake and fire. As Karl watched the rolling whiteness, he wished he could cover the ugliness that had overtaken his life—Enoch's death, separation from Tanny, and the slap of betrayal because his idol, Zachary, had drawn him into dishonest dealings. He was really in a mess. Without Zachary, he didn't even have a place to sleep.

As he trudged along his thoughts turned to God. "All things work together for good, Father. I got so tired of hearing Enoch say that. Can You really help things work out for me?" He paused on the curb as a wagon clattered past. "Enoch's gone. Tanny'll be gone tomorrow. I have no place to sleep, not even a blanket. Help me to understand how that's working things out."

Karl listened carefully, but God was silent as he plodded on. "All things work together for good. All things work together for good." He willed himself to believe it.

At last he neared the dock. The sight of Fish Willy sitting on his crate in the torch light, and hearing his cheerfully whistled tune brought things into perspective again. Karl hurried down the plank dock and squatted beside the old man. Willy stared into the darkness and didn't stir for a long time. Finally he pulled out his well-used handkerchief and blew his nose.

"That Zachary feller's been lookin' for you."

Karl's stomach lurched at the words and he patted Fish Willy's shoulders. "I'll be right back."

The speech he'd rehearsed buzzed through his brain like angry bees. As he approached, Zachary's head popped over the wagon side.

"You're late," Zachary called. "Where have you been?" Zachary jumped down from the wagon and without waiting for Karl's answer, talked on. "You'll need an early start tomorrow," he said. "I've promised too many moves but I've hired another driver and if we keep right at it I think we'll manage."

Karl sucked in his breath. "I won't be driving." Waves

120

lapped at the pilings beneath the pier. High overhead a gull called out, its lonely cry echoing against the dark hill behind them.

Zachary's eyes widened. "Nonsense! Like I said, I've promised."

Karl shoved his fists into his pockets to keep from punching Zachary. "I won't be driving for you anymore."

Zachary stared at Karl for a long moment, his jaw working. At long last his eyes narrowed and he shook his head. "Oh, I see. You want more money." With a shrug, he peeled another bill from his roll. A knowing smile settled upon his shrewd face and he gave a short laugh. "Looks like I taught you too well. You've got me over a barrel."

Zachary thrust the money toward Karl. The very act made Karl even angrier. "I don't want anything to do with you or your money!" he shouted. "Truth is, I don't believe in bilking honest folks."

Zachary's eyebrows climbed his forehead. "What do you mean by that?"

Karl closed the space between them. "Charging thirty dollars to move a poor man's few things. That's plain robbery."

Zachary's mouth twisted into a smirk. He grew defensive, sarcastic, "Looks like you've been around your Bible-thumping friend too long. There's lots of men that would give anything for your job and the good money it pays. Here I picked you up, an ignorant little farm boy, and gave you a chance to make it in the world. Then you shove it in my face. Well, if that's the way you want it that's the way you've got it, you ungrateful wretch. Looks like your late sidekick ruined you after all!"

Karl could handle Zachary's anger toward himself, but how *dare* he mock a dead boy. His hands leapt from his pockets and clenched into fists, fists that ached to smash the sneering face that wagged before him. He raised his arm, but then the memory of Enoch's gentle face rose between them, quietly nudging him in a different way.

Karl dropped his hands, then turned on his heel. Trembling with unspent anger, he marched down the dock to find Mr. Tweedy.

The kindly man greeted Karl with a hug. "You look upset, lad. Can I help?"

Karl fought for control. "I just quit working for Polson. Heard a couple things, and I don't have a stomach for what he's doin'."

Mr. Tweedy patted his shoulder. "Good for you, boy."

Karl looked up, "I was wondering if you could still use me."

It was like someone had extinguished lights in the old man's eyes. "Ah boy, I was hopin' you might change yer mind, but I'm afraid it's too late. I just hired me a man today. Waited long as I could, I'm sorry."

Those words were like a fist in Karl's gut. *"All things work together for good."*

"I understand," Karl said, turning to go. Mr. Tweedy grabbed Karl's arm. "Where'll you sleep tonight, lad?"

Karl shrugged.

"Then stay here with us until you find a better place." He pointed to the makeshift settlement on the dock—some wooden crates with canvas and horse blankets draped between them to ward off the mists. "We don't have much, but we're glad to share it."

Karl gulped. He glanced at the handful of unshaven men who huddled around the tiny fire. They were not lazy drifters, but men who had worked hard all their lives and had now lost everything in the earthquake. They were pulling together just to keep bread in their mouths, but they were willing to share what little they had.

Mr. Tweedy led Karl to the circle. Gratefully he accepted a

tin of hot soup to warm him. And that night he bedded down wrapped in one of Mr. Tweedy's horse blankets, right on the cold, hard pier.

The next Sunday the church was more crowded than ever. Heads nodded as the minister admonished the listeners to make—and keep—things right with God. Tears were shed over lost loved ones. Taking time to sit and really relax for the first time since the earthquake, Karl's regret and loneliness nearly choked him. He was glad when the service ended so he could turn his thoughts to other things.

On Monday morning Karl found work moving rubble from the streets. As he struggled to fill his wheelbarrow with brick and mortar and push it to the wagons which hauled it to the bay, he realized how lucky he had been to work for Mr. Tweedy at an easier job. City clean-up was sweaty, grueling toil and didn't pay as much as Mr. Tweedy had paid. But he needed the money, the work was necessary, and he determined to stick with it.

By Tuesday the news had spread all over town. Zachary and several other men who had been overcharging folks for their services had been arrested. Their wagons were confiscated and given to men willing to help others for a reasonable price. Karl shuddered. What would it have been like to be driving along, then stopped and arrested along with the others? Thankful that he had been spared such embarrassment, he sent a prayer heavenward, and worked all the harder.

Wednesday evening, just one week after the earthquake, Karl headed back to the dock after his long day's work. With a sigh he flopped down on his horseblanket to rest. Before long, Mr. Tweedy joined him.

"How's the new job?"

Karl groaned and held out his hands for his friend to inspect. Great red patches covered his palms—blisters broken from grasping wheelbarrow handles 12 hours a day.

123

"If I judged my future by today, I'd think all I did was trade moving manure for rubble," Karl said. "But it's OK. Actually, the foreman asked if I'd stay on after all the junk is gone and help rebuild a store." He grinned. "I guess that's pretty good."

Mr. Tweedy sighed. "It'll be a long time 'fore things get back to normal, lad, and it's going to take lots of strong, young fellers like you to put things back together. But we're thankful for our lives, ain't we?"

Karl thought of Enoch and Mr. Tweedy. "And friends who stand by us, no matter what."

Mr. Tweedy plunked his hand on Karl's shoulder. "Speaking of friends, someone came looking for you today." Weary men slowly walked back and forth on the dock as Karl's mind raced. Who could be looking for him? Surely not Tanny, though other than Zachary, she was the only one who knew where he was staying.

Just then footsteps stopped beside Karl. Karl stared at the man's boots—homemade boots with widely-spaced lace holes. Unable to believe his eyes, he whisked his gaze up the short body, his eyes finally resting on the most welcome grin he'd ever seen.

"You're alive!" Karl yelped, leaping to his feet and flinging his arms around Enoch.

"Always *have* been," mumbled Enoch, embarrassed by Karl's exuberance. "Fact is, I looked right regular fer yer name at The Registry'n just found it this afternoon. Were y' been, anyways?"

"Where've *I* been?" Karl shouted. "I thought you were buried under that old boarding house. I got there right after it went down and was sure you were a goner. But I kept checking at The Registry too. How'd you get out of that wreck, anyhow?"

As each boy told his story, the men who had shared their hospitality with Karl gathered around. Some of them had lost loved ones in the earthquake and it was good to be part of one happy ending.

"Funny thing," Enoch mused later as they sat together over cups of steaming soup, "but on th' quake mornin' I woke up early—y'know how I like t'sleep to th' last minute, but fer some reason I decided to head on out." He grinned in wonder. "I was in that little park when th' quake hit. I just stood there'n watched them buildin's tumble 'round my feet, like they was nothin' more then that bunch of board ends me 'n you use t' play with when we was little. Boy! It was awful!"

Karl couldn't believe his ears. "But you *never* wake up by yourself."

Enoch sobered as he looked out across the bay. "I know."

Goose bumps climbed Karl's arms. "Thank you, God," he said, realizing that even his unspoken prayers after the earthquake had been answered.

Right then the last shreds of disbelief left Karl. He knew without a doubt that God not only existed but He was a loving and caring heavenly Father. Tears filled his eyes but he didn't care. He and Enoch had survived the earthquake and would live to help rebuild San Francisco. God was very, very good.